CHICKEN SNAKE
&
CHUPACABRA COW

BRANDON BISHOP
&
BRANDON BISHIP JR.

Burning Bulb
PUBLISHING

Chicken Snake & Chupacabra Cow
By **Brandon Bishop and Brandon Bishop Jr.**

Burning Bulb Publishing
P.O. Box 4721
Bridgeport, WV 26330-4721
United States of America
www.BurningBulbPublishing.com

Second Edition.

Paperback Edition ISBN: 978-1-948278-71-3

CHAPTER 1
Farm Society and the Superstar

The bright, crisp, flowing wheat, the blinding sun flickering through the windmill blades, the ever-rusting broken tractor resting forever in a shallow grave ditch where it harvested its final grain. The symphony of the residents calling out in various tones and voices. The contrast of the peeling red paint to the endless green fields, the dust clouds following the rare sight of a passing neighbor driving down the dirt road. Yep, it's a typical farm to passersby. Still, if you look a little closer, you'll learn that this farm society isn't much different than any other society, even the very one that you live in.

There's a government and leaders; everyone has their job and purpose, and rules and regulations need to be followed to make the whole system work. There are mothers, fathers and children, grandparents, aunts and uncles and cousins, dear close friends and bitter enemies, undeniable love and extreme dislikes, heated drama and lasting happiness, life, death, and everything in between. And much like in your society, there are those who stand out.

Some might call them celebrities or superstars. Some stand out for their unique talents, some for the way they look or dress, some have a savvy business sense that puts them in the public eye, but others just have that special something, an IT factor that draws adoration. When it comes to the one they call "Chicken Snake," it was a little bit of everything.

The entire farm was in awe of Chicken Snake. Imagine seeing your all-time favorite movie or TV star, musician, or historical figure; imagine seeing them in person. That's what it was like when Chicken Snake walked by. But deep inside, Chicken Snake felt as though he was just another member of the farm community. "Oh, my goodness!" A group consisting of a cow, a pig, and two chickens squealed. "Could you autograph my feathers!" Yelled one of the chickens. "My snout,

MY SNOUT! Could you initial it!" said the hefty pig. "My kids love you, Chicken Snake!" Yelled the cow.

"Guys! Guys! Please, I mean, I appreciate it, but I'm no different than anyone else here. I just happen to be half chicken and half snake. I know it's weird and different, but please, please…" Chicken Snake calmly replied to their fanatic outbursts. Just then, as it seemed to happen on a daily basis, the crowd got bigger and bigger. Everyone from the field mice to the horses, the crows to the sheep, from insects to the farmer's dogs chimed in and hung on every word coming from his beak.

"Hey everyone, I think Chicken Snake is going to tell us the story again!" And then the crowd got even bigger.

"Oh, not again. Come on! You all know the story. How many times do I have to do this?"

"Just one more time, Chicken Snake!" yelled a mouse in a super high voice.

"Yeah, one more time! One more time!"

Chicken Snake shook his head slowly with a blank face as the "One more time!" chant grew louder and louder.

"Okay, Okay! ONE LAST TIME!" he responded, knowing that it would be far from the last time he told this story. A happy roar fired back at him from his excited audience.

"Yes!"

"Impressive!"

"Quiet everybody, he's telling the story!"

The crowd was giddy for the story they'd heard countless times, and a hush fell over the field. Chicken Snake adjusted his tie. Yes, he was known for wearing very nice ties. He flapped his wings, hopped up onto the back of a hay wagon, and cleared his throat.

"Ahem, okay, Here's the story of how I became Chicken Snake… again…"

Captivated glassy eyes and slightly hung open mouths all leaned inward as Chicken Snake started from the very beginning. "Years ago, my mom was a simple hen on this farm, just like the hundreds that live here today. She spent her days feeding on grain and her evenings laying eggs in the henhouse. From what I've heard, she was a lovely soul everyone enjoyed being around, but she also had a mischievous, adventurous side that often got her into trouble. Once, she stole a pack of markers from the farmer's desk and colored her neighbor's eggs all different colors, even drawing smiley faces on some of them. It confused the entire farm. That poor neighbor chicken spent days being medically evaluated; they still never figured out why she was laying green and purple eggs." Chicken Snake laughed with his crowd.

Another time, my mother broke out of the henhouse at night and flapped into the front yard where the Farmer's dogs were sleeping.

Apparently, there was one particular dog named Dale who would always harass the feeding chickens. He'd bark out threats from the other side of the fence, such as "Hey, you Chickens! You're all lucky this fence is here. If it weren't, I'd be eating chicken nuggets every day!" So, as you can imagine, he freaked them out as they were trying to grab a bite. Well, my mom felt as though she had to do something, and she certainly wasn't about to allow that mutt to continue making life miserable for her fellow chickens any longer.

So, on a cool, quiet October night (actually, I've been told it was Halloween night), my mom silently crept into the front yard wearing a white sack she found in the barn, holding a megaphone and a cattle prod.

"I hate cattle prods!" said an older cow in the crowd.

"Yeah, I can imagine you would," said Chicken Snake. "My Mom inched closer and closer to Dale's dog house, where she could hear him snoring loudly. She looked out of the two eye holes she cut in the white sack and made her way around to the back of the dog house. She found a small hole in the wood and gently placed the cattle prod an inch away from Dale's dog butt, and turned it on. She then made her way to the front of the old dog house, turned the megaphone up to maximum volume, and screamed into it.

"I am the ghost of the angry chicken!!!"

Of course, Dale jumped out of sleep and backed into the cattle prod. It zapped his posterior, and he yelped loud enough to wake up the entire farm, including the Farmer!

"The Angry Chicken demands that you never EVER even look at the chickens on this farm again!!!"

The dog jumped backward again and again, zapped himself, and went into a barking frenzy.

"If you do not obey the Ghost of the Angry Chicken, I shall return!"

Just then, my mom lunged forward at Dale, and yet again, he backed into the shocking cattle prod and screamed. The porch light then came on, and the Farmer began looking out the screen door window.

"Dale? You, okay?"

She grabbed the prod, flew back over the fence, and returned to her nesting bed in the henhouse without being seen. Dale, the Farmer's dog, was hardly ever the same again. He was scarred for life and never even once made eye contact with any chicken ever again. Today, he spends most of his time inside the Farmer's house." Laughter spread across Chicken Snake's audience; even the Farmer's other dogs were chuckling a bit.

"But my mom's luck ran out one day. Instead of joining the others during feeding time, she decided she wanted to see more of the farm. She had lived there her entire life and only knew of a couple of small areas. She could see the endless crops. She could see the horses roaming free, the trees in the distance, and other Farmers in those large moving metal boxes with wheels coming and going. She wanted to know where they went, where they were going. So again, she hopped over the short wire fence and set out on an adventure sparked by curiosity and a thirst to learn more about the farm. She thought, "Are there other farms? Other henhouses? Maybe other animals I've never seen?"

She was nervous but mostly excited. She reached the dirt road in front of the farm, and she looked back at the farm and realized it looked very small compared to what lay ahead. There's an old joke in chicken lore that goes, "Why did the chicken cross the road?" Well, at first, she was crossing the road to simply get to the other side, but something caught her eye in the grass by the mailbox, and THAT is why she crossed. As she got closer and closer, she heard a hissing noise. She'd never heard anything like it before.

"Hello? Is there someone, err...something there?"

The whole point of her adventure was to find new friends and see new places, but she never imagined it would happen so quickly. Just then, a long-looking figure revealed itself from the grass-filled ditch on the side of the dirt road. My mom was startled but very interested.

"Ssssooo, Ssssomeone Ssssnuck away from the Farm…" IT said.

"Who are you? What are you?" my mom said.

"Sssssimon's the name, and a Sssssnake is what I am."

"Well, hello, Simon, I'm a chicken; I'm from the farm behind me."

"No, I don't believe that'sss accurate." Said Simon the Snake. "Whatever could you mean? That's exactly who I am and where I'm from."

6

"No, no, no, no, no," the Snake said with a sinister calm and a piercing half smile as he slid closer to my mom. "That may have been who you were and where you were from…" He said while moving slowly inch by inch closer to my mom.

"What you are now is my DINNER, and HERE is your new home!!!" Simon the Snake lunged ferociously as other chickens still on the farm began watching this horrific scene from behind the fence. Simon missed with his first attempt but quickly coiled his body around her and tried again and again. My mom was able to break free each time as Simon wasn't a large snake at all; as a matter of fact, she was way bigger than he was, but he was powerful and relentless and had fangs like daggers. My mom ran back towards the farm. The other chickens and all the animals frantically screamed in unison. "Hurry, he's right behind you!"

"RUN! RUN! You're almost home!"

My mom was just a few yards from the fences, and the snake kept lunging time and time again within inches of her. She got to the fence and flapped her wings in a frenzy, and she was almost to safety, but…"

Chicken Snake had to stop for a moment. Even though he's told this story over a hundred times, he still gets choked up when telling this particular part.

"It's okay, Chicken Snake," yelled someone from the crowd. "You don't have to go on. We know the rest."

"No, No, it's alright. I've come this far in the story; I have to finish now."

Chicken Snake cleared his throat again, readjusted his tie, wiped a tear from his eye, and moved forward.

"My mom was inches away from being home and safe on the farm, but as she jumped over the fence, that Snake also made one final strike. This time, he got her… but it wasn't over yet.

"Like I said, the snake was much smaller than my mom. Snakes can open their mouths very wide, but in this case, not nearly wide enough. My mom was hurt, very hurt, actually… she was dying… but in a strange case of poetic justice and karma.

Simon the Snake was also in trouble. He was stuck. The Snake couldn't release his fangs, he couldn't swallow, and he eventually died while my mom was still conscious. Moments later, still with the snake's mouth engulfing her entire back half, whether it was out of fear or maybe it was just time, my mom laid two eggs. Of course, the eggs were laid inside the snake, unbeknownst to any onlookers trying to separate the chicken and the snake. She also died moments later. Now, I don't know much about science or nature; I don't know any more or less than anyone here. But somehow, those eggs rested and incubated within Simon the Snake for weeks. Even though the snake was deceased, the eggs stayed healthy. When my mother was finally separated from the snake, she was given a proper ceremony. Everyone on the farm was there. I was told it was beautiful.

"It was, I was there." mentioned a horse standing over the rest of the listeners. It wasn't such a glorious occasion for Simon the Snake. His body lied next to the fence, and no one looked twice. But inside, there was plenty going on. One day, the nearby crows began feasting on what used to be Simon. I know that's gross, but it's how the world works. We all know that all too well, don't we?

"We sure do." grumbled the pigs. From what I've been told, those crows kept digging until they found the two eggs inside, and they grabbed one of them and flew away; the other chickens found the other egg and took it to the henhouse, where it soon after hatched.

Again, I can't explain how or why this happened. It really makes zero sense, but all I can tell you is that it happened, and I'm living proof of it.

When that egg cracked open, everyone gathered around to see a chicken pop its head out. Everyone gasped with joy. They functioned as if it were a miracle. But the cheer turned to shock as the shell continued to break away. Piece by piece fell into the hay below, slowly revealing something that had never been seen before or since.

Not only did a healthy, happy baby chick hatch that day, but its lower half was long, scaly, and green. Somehow, someway, for some reason, it was half chicken and half snake. (It was ME! And I'll go through this world as Chicken Snake for as long as I'm here.)

It never ceased to amaze Chicken Snake that he gets the same thrilled gasps and looks of wonder and amazement EVERY time he tells the story.

"But once again, PLEASE understand. None of this means I'm any different than anyone here. I'm not special by any means. I'm just a part of this community, just like you."

"Well, not really. I mean, you're half chicken and half snake. That's... uh... amazing!" said a robin that flew in for the storytelling.

"I understand I'm a little different, but please, just treat me like anyone else." "Okay Check Snake... But I'd still like that autograph!" Obliviously, the pig spoke out. "Yeah, can I get a selfie with you?"

Another voice blurted out, "Hey! Chicken Snake! Wanna get some grain?", etcetera, etcetera. The farm society had already made up their minds; Chicken Snake was a celebrity, He was their hero, and they weren't going to allow his humble wishes to be, well, HUMBLE to distract them from their fandom.

But there was someone in the back that kept quiet; he never missed Chicken Snake telling the story. He was certainly a huge fan, but instead of taking in an emotional, inspirational story of overcoming loss and beating the odds, he noticed the others in the crowd and saw that look of admiration. He saw them flock to wherever he was and hang on his every word. Maybe, just maybe, he'd like a little of that for himself.

He was a cow...not just an ordinary cow...but a... well, no, he was certainly an ordinary cow.

But not for long.

CHAPTER 2
A Cow with a Story of His Own

The funny thing about cows is that they don't really have names. No, really… they just simply call each other "Cow."

Casual greetings go along the lines of, "Hey Cow!" "Oh, hey, Cow!" "How's your day, Cow?"

While humans separate them by gender and breed, sometimes calling them Steers, Bulls, Heifers, even Ox or even Moo Moo, in cow society, they keep it simple: it's just "Cow."

The Cow we're talking about has spent his entire life on the farm. He looked a lot like the other cows and did all the normal cow things. He mooed, grazed, and tended to his duties around the barn. For the most part, he kept to himself, a dreamer, always searching for knowledge, always listening to the stories shared by others. Still, he had no stories of his own. He wanted to stand out, be on the back of that hay wagon with everyone on the farm glued to his every word, invested in his sagas and journeys.

Still, outside of grazing for hours daily and sleeping standing up, he really did not have much to say. Sometimes, he would see flying vehicles in the sky. They disappear and reappear around the clouds in straight lines chased by trails of clouds. But everyone sees those, and he had no idea what they were, so that wouldn't work or be very interesting.

He constantly thought to himself, "I need an angle. I need that special something that sets me apart from not only the other cows but from everyone on the farm."

Sometimes, he sees his reflection in the water tub. He moves around and checks out his every angle.

"Maybe I look different? Maybe I have extremely attractive cow legs that no one will be able to resist?" He thought. "Nope… as a matter of fact, amazing cow legs look exactly like every other cow's legs I've ever seen." "Oh wait! The black spot on my left side kind of looks like that cloud up in the sky! I mean, it's uncanny how similar it is! I have to tell the entire farm! Hey! HEY! Everyone! Come here quick!" A couple of his fellow cows gathered around.

"Okay, guys, look at my left side. See my black spot?" he excitedly stumbles the word out.

"Yeah?" replied another cow.

"Okay, well, look up at that cloud and... tell me it doesn't... look... like..." the words left his following sentence as he noticed that the cloud had already disappeared.

"What are we looking at, Cow?" they asked.

"Nothing... Nothing at all, I guess. Sorry, I thought I... well, never mind..."

The other cows hoofed their way back to grazing, and Cow stood blank-faced and drained of the excitement he was about to share.

"Even the clouds don't find me all that special. Oh well..." He wandered away from the water tub and went back to being another ordinary cow, grazing in an ordinary field on another ordinary day.

Later that night, Cow was standing out in his field in the middle of a deep sleep. He was having a nightmare about the dreaded and infamous Cow Tippers. The Cow Tippers might have only been a legend told by elders for as long as he can remember, but they told the story well, and just about every cow on the farm believed they existed.

In his dream, they drew closer; there were so many of them. He wondered why they were looking solely at him. Why, with such evil grins and glares like daggers in their eyes.

"Why are the humans so cruel? What could they possibly gain from pushing me over?" he thought. They got closer with their hands reaching out in a push position. They gained speed; he was frozen and unable to run or scream. Just inches away.

"NOOO!!!"...

His eyes opened to the dark of night. A galaxy of sparkling stars welcomed him back to reality. A nice cool breeze washed over his face, and the familiar buzzing of flies over the compost filled his ears like a symphony.

"Oh, man! I hate that dream."

It wasn't the first time he had that dream, and he knew, without a doubt, it wouldn't be the last. He looked around the farm, the starlit sky, the flames flickering inside lanterns placed throughout the grounds, even inside the barn and the Farmer's house. Sometimes, he'd count the lanterns just to make sure the Farmer stayed on top of his duties.

At this moment, he felt alone, but in a good way. It was quiet, dark, a perfect night. Outside of crickets and distant owls, everyone was silent and slumbering.

"This is nice…" he quietly muttered. He started to think about his life on the farm.

"I'm bored with this. I'm just bored with doing the same thing day after day after day." His thoughts aggressively rambled. "When will it be my time? I don't want to just be another cow. There's no way I was born to graze and do simple random tasks around the old barn. I'm somebody. There has to be a special purpose for me. I mean, what does Chicken Snake have that I don't have?"

He pondered for a few moments, almost working himself into a fit until he calmly thought, "Well, he's a chicken and a snake. THAT'S who he is. And I guess that IS rather spectacular." He laughed aloud a bit. And with that chuckle, it seemed to have released an entirely new avenue of thought. He swore he saw a lightbulb shine above his horns.

"What if I were also a hybrid of sorts. Yeah! He's half chicken and half snake. What if I was half cow and…um… half cow and…" his thought process immediately fell to pieces.

"Well, I'm not. I'm 100% cow."

But the rush of invention once again crept up inside of him.

"Well, no one knows for sure that I'm all cow. I wasn't born here; no one knows my past. I never knew my parents. Who knows what I am?"

His excitement plastered a huge smile on his face.

"I can be whatever I want to be!"

All of a sudden, his life was a blank canvas, and he felt like he had every color of the rainbow at his disposal. He thought, "Well, I'm obviously a cow. Let's just say I got that from my mother. But my father, he was a… uh, he was a … A RABBIT! Yes, a rabbit!" He thought he could pull it off. He stuck his two front teeth out and began hopping all over the field.

"Dude! Cow! Knock it off!" another Cow whispered, "You woke me up with all that jumping around, and you look like an idiot. Go back to sleep!"

"Well, maybe not…" he thought. "Okay, okay, half cow, half cow, half…hmmm… Kitty Cat! Yeah, somehow, my father was of the feline persuasion." He saw cats running all over the farm, but what characteristics could he possibly add to his personality that proved he was half-kitty?

"They PURR! Yeah! Once, a little orange kitty cat was brushing through my cow legs. It made a soft rumbling sound. It was very pleasant. I asked her what that noise was, and she said, "Well, I'm purring silly." So, if I could only learn to purr, then everyone would believe that I'm a cat cow."

He loved the sound of that. Almost sounded like a superhero. He thought that everyone would line up at the hay wagon for stories told by the fantastic CAT COW. "So how does one purr?" He wondered. "It's like a rumble. A low, deep, happy rumble... Hmmm... WAIT! My stomach makes that noise when I'm hungry! Maybe I AM half cat! This is unbelievable!"

Cow wasn't starving by any means. Actually, after grazing all day, he wasn't even the slightest bit hungry. "

Maybe if I just tighten up my whole body and squeeze my stomach muscles, then maybe the purring will begin. It HAS to work!" Just then, Cow strained and tightened his stomach muscles, and his face began to turn red. He grimaced and pushed himself to make that cat-like rumble. His face took on a purple tint. Every muscle in his large cow body was straining, and then...

"Pfffffft!" Well, he farted... loudly.

The other cows were startled and woke.

"Cow! What was that? Man!" The annoyed cows began to stir and comment.

"Are you kidding me, Cow?"

"Methane alert for this part of town."

They took turns making jokes.

"Hey, put a cork in it! "

"No air biscuits allowed out here! Geez Cow!"

"Someone's making cow patties!"

"Gross, point that thing downwind!"

"Wow, even the flies don't like that smell, eew!"

This went on for a little while. Cow figured he'd get some sleep and think more of what he'd like to be in the morning.

"Hey Cow... Did you hear about ninja farts? They're silent but deadly! Haha!"

"What's invisible and smells like bananas? A monkey fart! Haha!"

"Hey, why do trees stink? Cause their Farmer CUT ONE… Haha!"

"Okay, guys, I get it! Go to sleep!"

The next morning was windy. The wheat stood sideways. Leaves leaped into the air into funnel shapes that then scattered across the fields. The old rusty bell clanged back and forth. Cow loved it. He knew it would be cold in a few months; he remembered how insanely hot it was just a few months ago. A little dust in the eyes and messed up hair was just fine in comparison. He approached a group of fellow cows.

"It's a little windy out today," he mentioned, hoping to launch a casual conversation.

"Yeah, it was even windier last night, Cow." One of them joked.

"Oh, come on guys, we're cows. We all break wind. It's what we do!" he reasoned.

"Break wind? The wind almost broke all of us last night!" Haha!"

They all laughed and then scattered throughout the fields for breakfast.

"Ugh…" he thought. "This is just great. Now, instead of being a complete nobody, I am now I'm The Amazing Farting Cow, lovely." But Cow got right back on track. He knew he was onto something last night. He just had to figure out exactly what his other half was going to be. He thought in rapid fire, "A Chipmunk! No, too small… A Lion! No, I look nothing like the Lions… Maybe a Dog! Gah, the Farmer's dogs would sniff that one right out." His mind raced. He couldn't stand being just an ordinary farm cow any longer. What was it going to be?

"Half cow. Half human! Ugh, no way, gross… Eagle… Pig… Spider…Eww! People would hate me… um… Sheep… Bunny, No, I already said that… uhhh… Giraffe… Rhino… Elephant… Turkey… No, those are stupid ideas! I AM HALF COW and HALF… Umm… Umm… "and just then, out of nowhere, a newspaper flew into the field and draped itself over Cow's entire head.

"MOO!" he yelled as it completely freaked him out.

During windstorms, trash often found its way onto the farm, stuff from cities miles and miles away. It's basically how they knew a larger world even existed. It's how rumors got started and creepy legends like "The Cow Tippers" were born.

He felt lucky. Usually, he heard these stories from others who received these gifts from the great beyond, but it's his turn today. He held down the paper with both front hoofs and scanned it for the first thing he thought might be interesting.

"This is great! I can soak in all of these stories and share everything with the rest of the farm. Finally, they'll see me. They'll hear what I have to say! I'm not The Amazing Farting Cow, I'm not just an ordinary everyday nobody, I'm The Bringing of News! The Storyteller from the Great Unknown Lands!"

His eyes raced across the black and white pages. "The Weekly Observer," he read. He learned of Aliens flying over Mexico, about a great earthquake under a place called New York City. He thought, "Not sure what an earthquake is or where New York City is, but I hope they're okay." He read about a new virus that was about to wipe out the population by making people sneeze until they exploded.

This is crazy!" Cow thought, "What a messed up world it is out there!" His eyes then focused on a blurry picture in the bottom right corner of the page.

"The deadly Arizona Chupacabra harasses a small town, caught on tape."

"What's a Chupacabra?" he thought. "This vicious beast was once thought to be mythical, but The Weekly Observer cameras stayed vigilant while roaming the small town streets in Arizona, which have been under Marshall Law since their attacks began, and we captured proof that it not only exists but the Chupacabra is on the hunt!"

He read while moving his lips to every word.

"Chupacabra... that's it! I can almost feel Chupacabra blood coursing through my veins. It's perfect. Chicken Snake has his lovable Chicken side but also the frightening and intimidating Snake half. I'll have my normal adorable and friendly cow half, but deep inside me lies the heart and the mending soul of the dreadful ferocious Chupacabra!"

Cow stood firmly with his chest puffed out, his legs forming a powerful foundation, and with a stern confident look upon his face, he roared, "Yesterday I was yet a mere ordinary cow, but today, yes today I... AM... CHUPACABRA COW!"

He remained in that pose for maybe just a few moments too long... Just a tad too long...

"Hey! Everyone gather around! Seriously, Come on! Get everyone to meet me by the hay wagon! Let's go!" Cow frantically amassed a crowd. He hoped for a crowd the size of a Chicken Snake story session, but he was happy to gather what he could get with such short notice.

"This is it! This is my big moment! No turning back now." He managed to put together a nice-sized audience by the wagon he had always envisioned himself upon. He knew they'd be riveted with his new revelation. It was every bit as incredible as Chicken Snake's.

"Life is about to change for the better," he said as he pumped himself up and climbed up onto the podium like a hay wagon.

"What's this about Cow?" the horse in attendance asked bluntly.

"Yeah, we've got a lot of mud to Roll around in and slop too much on. What's going on?" the pigs asked while chewing loudly on who knows what.

Cow scanned the crowd. He saw the curiosity. He saw many of the same faces that absorbed everything said by Chicken Snake. He knew that he'd soon be met with the same respect, the same adoration and awe.

"Thank you all for coming! I have a crazy... no, an amazing... no, an UNBELIEVABLE story to share with you all!"

"We already know about the fart Cow. The whole farm knows about it," blurted out one of the Farmer's dogs.

"Okay, enough about that. Let it go already!" Cow responded.

"How about you STOP letting it go!"

The crowd erupted in laughter.

Cow stood there annoyed until the laughter died down. "Are you done?" he asked with dry emotion. "Just listen... I have recently discovered that I'm not just your everyday ordinary cow." he happily announced.

"What's wrong with being a normal cow?" the other cows asked. "Well, nothing. Of course, there's nothing wrong with being a cow, but I'm only half cow!"

"You look like a normal everyday cow to us," said a voice from the back. "Yes, I know, I LOOK like a standard cow, but running through my veins is the blood of the rare and dreaded CHUPACABRA!" Cow said in a spookier tone.

"What's a Cup-of-Crapa?" asked a squirrel.

"I just told you! It's a vicious monster that roams the planet and terrorizes entire towns! My mother was a cow, and my father was a sinister Chupacabra. And I... Yes, I AM CHUPACABRA COW!"

Once again, he struck that same power stance as he announced his new moniker, this time in front of half the farm community. His eyes proudly clasped shut, his smile brand and without hesitation. In his mind, the crowd was standing quietly in awe, waiting for his next words, but when he opened his eyes…

"Where's everybody going?"

The crowd was half gone, and the rest were heading back to their daily farm responsibilities.

"What? Wait? Where are you going? I'm Chupacabra Cow! I haven't even started my story yet! Wait!"

"What proof do you have?" asked a hawk perched next to him on the wagon.

"What? Proof?" a confused and disappointed Cow replied.

"Yeah, proof. You can't just announce that you're half monster without proof."

"I never said I was half monster. I said half Chupacabra. Why do I need proof? Why won't you just simply take my word?"

The Hawk smirked. "Sorry, Cow, but you're not going to convince too many people of anything without a shred of proof. Good luck with your silly little fairy tale. See you around, weirdo!"

"Well, that didn't go like I thought it would." Cow's hopes were shattered. He thought by this point, he'd be captivating a crowd of his peers. They'd immediately start spreading legendary rumors of his heroic half-Chupacabra existence, maybe even writing songs. But nope. Instead, he's standing on the hay wagon, looking out at a crowd of no one. He took shameful steps off the wagon and headed into the barn. He knew this barn so well that he never had to even look where he was headed. After all, he has spent his entire life in that barn or the fields, just an everyday, ordinary cow. And he was beginning to let that fact settle in that it's all he will ever be.

As soon as he entered the barn, he heard something clapping their hands from the farther dark corner.

"Good Job Cow! Or should I say, Chupacabra Cow!"

It was Chicken Snake!

"Oh my gosh! It's really him!" Cow thought as he fixed his hair and stomped the mud off his feet.

"Calm down, Cow, It's just me. I thought you did great up there. Don't let those close-minded cattle get you down. None of them could have ever done what you just did. They're sheep!"

"I heard that…" said an unseen sheep in the barn, who then slowly walked out.

"Never mind them, Cow. It was a great story. I'd love to hear more." "Well, thanks, Mr. Chicken Snake, sir…" he nervously rambled.

"Look, just call me Chicken Snake. Actually, my true friends call me Chake. You know, like "Ch" from chicken and "ake" from snake. But only call method if you plan on being a pal."

"Absolutely! What an honor, Chicke- err, Chake!"

"And since we're flapping our wings, what would you like me to call you?" asked Chake.

"Um, maybe Chow? You know, like "Ch" from Chupacabra & "ow" from Cow?" Cow said.

"Kid, do you really want to be on a cattle farm and named after something the Farmer called dinner?"

"Good point." Cow realized quickly.

"I'll just call you Chupacabra Cow until we think of something else. It's got a nice ring to it. So, tell me your story. Who cares if I'm the only one who hears it for now? Soon, you'll be a legend, kid! I mean, I've read about those Chupacabras in the wind trash. You must be a really vicious creature under that leather." Shake put Cow over. "And don't let them discourage you with proof. What is proof anyway? Someone's proof is another's lie, and someone's lie is another's proof. Your word is what matters to me. Do you think anyone would believe that I was half snake if I didn't have this long, scaly tail?" asked Chake.

"I imagine it would be a hard sale," added Cow.

"Exactly. Well, let's go get some chow, Chow… Haha!" They both shared a laugh and voyaged out to the windy field.

"So, A Chupacabra eh?" Chake broke open the conversation while pecking at some grain. "I thought being half snake was crazy enough."

"Yeah, it's… something…" Cow said with some hesitation. Cow knew that the hawk was right. He had no proof. He wondered what he himself would think if someone else came out with this insane story of being half Chupacabra without a lick of evidence. He'd probably think they were insane and dismiss even the possibility of such a claim, much like the rest of the farm had done to him.

Yet, he also has no proof that he's NOT half Chupacabra.

"That's very true…" he said aloud.

"What's that?" asked Chake.

"Oh, nothing, Chake. Just thinking out loud."

All of a sudden, the wind picked up even more. Everyone began gathering inside the big red barn. The Farmer took control of the shutters on his house with a loud thud for each. The fences started to sway in the stiff breeze, the lanterns outside swung back and forth, and their flames blew out. The barn filled up to maximum capacity. Suddenly, a bright flash of lightning illuminated the entire farm, followed by a deafening crack of thunder. It startled even the most stoic of creatures. Drop by drop, the rain began to fall. It wasn't the worst storm they'd seen, but it certainly made everyone grateful for the warm safety of the old barn.

CHAPTER 3

The Barn, a Storm and a New Story

The Old Red Barn was constructed before any of its current residents were born, quite possibly even older than The Farmer himself. It stood like a beacon between the towering rusted silver silo and the constantly creaking windmill. With its peeling red paint and large doors that would swing with the wind, there's no place on the farm where it escaped your sight. Whether you were a chicken or cow, pig or horse, or even the owls, cats, and field mice that found their way, it was home to all.

Everyone had seen much worse storms than this one, which continued into the night. But they were always concerned about the Old Red Barn. With every powerful gust of wind, they could feel it sway. The tired wood chopped down a century ago would sound like it was about to snap into a million splinters. They gathered and watched through small windows as the water tub fell from its stand and the hay brushed from the wagon and into the sky.

"Look at The Farmer!" a Horse said. With one hand holding down his hat, the Farmer was snuffing out lanterns outside his house and closing the shutters before heading back inside. Everyone huddled together inside; for the most part, they were separated by small fences, horses in one area, cows in another, and so on. But when the big storms hit, it brought them as close together as they could possibly be.

One time, a few years back, a giant spinning cloud that reached from the ground to the sky ripped right through the farm. It almost took The Barn down. Doors were ripped off the hinges, windows shattered, Farm equipment was easily thrown around, and even the windmill was shredded into pieces. The Farmer quickly built a new one, but no one had ever forgotten that day. It only lasted a few minutes, but it seemed like an eternity. Half the fencing around The Farm was pulled from the ground and thrown for miles around. Pieces of the fence actually hit the Barn and broke some windows. But the

Barn held firm, and ever since that day, everyone trusted it to keep them safe.

The barn was warm, the roof showed no leaks, and everyone was safe and dry. The strong winds outside would creep in and wash over those inside, but it felt kind of nice. The inside of The Barn was lit up by a single lantern hanging from the ceiling where Chicken Snake, realizing that no one was ready to fall asleep anytime soon, flapped up on a hay bale and figured he'd provide entertainment until the storm blew over.

"Hey, everyone! CHICKEN SNAKE!" they all said in unison, at once forgetting the weather. This woke up Chupacabra Cow, who was seemingly the only one able to fall asleep during the storm. He yawned and staggered over to see what the commotion was about.

"Tell the story! Tell the story!" they chanted and begged as usual.

"No, no, no, not tonight," he replied. "Besides, you already know the story. I literally just gave you my story like yesterday. Today, we're going to hear a NEW story, which happened right here on The Farm."

"Is it the story about how a Chicken became half snake??" blurted out a goat.

"Everybody focus! Just listen to what I'm saying here! No, it's not my story. It's even better!"

Everyone was taken aback. A BETTER story than the greatest story they've ever heard? Now he had their attention.

"Okay, this happened years ago. Some of the facts are a little blurry because it happened so long ago, but I'll tell you this: I believe it."

Well, if Chicken Snake, the most popular member of this Farm Society, believes it, then the rest of them really had no choice. They were down to soak in every single word as truth.

"This story is about someone who might seem as though he's just like everyone else, but under his hide, he's truly a wonder. Now, we all know that quite often on The Farm, we have to say our goodbyes. The big truck comes, they load up some friends and family, and they're taken to the Amazing Great Farm, where life is even better than it is here. We all know this. I mean, I THINK we all know this… Either way, someday, we all hope to go to that special Great Farm ourselves and see all of our friends, but that's another story entirely.

Back to the story. Many moons ago, a cow was loaded onto the truck; she was one of the very best milkers on the farm; for years, she made a name for herself by out-producing every other milking cow by gallons.

After a lifetime of good work, she was finally rewarded, and they let her retire and live out her days relaxing on beautiful pastures and grazing at The Great Farm. But that's not what happened. It was a cold, icy winter day when the truck pulled away onto the dirt road. Only a few miles from here, the big truck hit a large chunk of ice and slid into a small lake. The human driver managed to escape, but everyone in the back didn't make it out of the frozen river… except one.

The Cow managed to escape the truck trailer when it crashed at the bottom of the river, and the lock broke. She kicked her legs vigorously and managed to float her way to the frigid air, but she was still in trouble. Her hoofs kept sliding off the muddy banks for the river. She grew tired of trying to pull herself out of the water. She had never been so cold. Just when she was about to give up and sink back down to the bottom of the freezing river, she felt a tug. Someone or something was pulling on her tail. At this point, she was nearly unconscious. The cold had robbed her of any ability to speak or even think straight. The last thing she remembered before passing out was the feel of grass and rocks against her side as she was being dragged onto land and seeing four furry legs through her blurry eyes."

Chicken Snake has the crowd hooked, as he always does. The storm raged on outside, but no one paid any attention to it. The Barn could've begun to fall apart piece by piece at this point, and all anyone would care about was what happened to the cow after she was pulled from the river. Who pulled her from the river? Chake knew how to capture the attention of everyone in the room. They were locked in.

"Just then…" Chake said in a low tone. "SHE WOKE UP!"

The crowd gasped and screeched a bit. Chake did this on purpose because he thought giving them a loud jolt would be funny, and it was.

"She woke up in the shell of a broken-down barn in the middle of nowhere. She must've been dragged for miles. She could no longer see the river, the road, or… who brought her to this place. She stood up, still very sore from the crash, and scraped up and stinging from the ground after being dragged. She stumbled outside of this skeleton frame of a barn from centuries ago. She was no longer cold but shivered when she realized she was lost and alone. But she wasn't alone. 'I was going to eat you,' said a deep, growling voice from behind her. She quickly turned around, grimacing in pain from sore ribs.

"Who are you? WHAT are you?" she asked in a panic.

"I'm the one who saved you from a frozen death in that river," said the sinister yellow-eyed creature.

"You wanted to eat me? What do you mean? I'm not Hay, or Grain, or Slop. I'm a cow! You can't eat a cow!" she naively replies.

Cow spent her entire life on the farm. They ate what The Farmer gave them; she had never imagined that cows could possibly be food.

"Settle down, I'm not going to eat you. Lucky for you, I'm quite full. You see, there's a small town just a few blocks over full of humans. I love terrorizing humans. They were so afraid of me that they all packed up and moved away. So now I've got the whole place to myself, all the food and comforts I could ever need."

"What's a town? Do you mean the Farm? What are Humans?" she cluelessly asked.

"You've got to be kidding me," he said with a confused look on his face.

"I've never been off The Farm. All I know is that I was heading to The Great Farm, the truck crashed, and now I'm… I'm just scared…"

She started to cry. Her teardrops nearly froze by the time they reached her cheeks.

"Stop it, there's no crying out here. You won't make it another day if you're weak. Thicken your hide, girl, and follow me. I'm gonna show you a whole new world."

Chupacabra Cow nudged his way to the middle of the crowd and made eye contact with Chake. He smiled, and Chake smiled back. He still wasn't entirely sure where this story was going, but with every word he said, he began to realize exactly where this was going.

"So, the creature and the cow wandered off into the chilly night with nothing but dirt and rock beneath their steps and each other for conversation. It wasn't a short path to where he was taking her, so they became well-versed in each other's stories.

"You never told me your name or exactly what you are," she asked as if she'd been waiting awhile to know.

"Name? When you're a feared creature that strikes panic into the hearts and minds of man, you don't need a name. They just call me what I am, a Chupacabra…" Just then, Chupacabra Cow made a high-pitched "eek!" sound that he'd never made before. A few around him looked at him with puzzled faces. He now knew for a fact that Chake was telling the entire Farm his story. Funny enough, he was also hearing it for the first time.

"Wait… How does he know my story?" he thought. But that didn't matter. He was as curious as the rest of the Barn to hear what's next.

"A Chupacabra? Is that like some kind of Farmer's dog?" The Cow asked. "

A Dog? Haha!" he chuckled. "Have you ever seen a dog this big? I could eat ten dogs for lunch!" he boasted.

"Please don't do that. I have several friends that are dogs," she pleaded. "Calm yourself! I'm just kidding.! You have a lot to learn, girl, and this is where your learning begins." He said as they both saw the outline of a small town in the distance.

"I call it Chupacabra City! Population ME!" he proudly announced. "Just a few weeks ago, there were about 200 humans living here. All I had to do was walk up and down the street a few times and chase a few of their bratty kids around, and what do you know. They all moved away," he explains as they walk side by side down the middle of the main street. "Sure, they tried to hunt me down; they even set up traps, but nothing worked. I'm too good. I'd hide in the shadows and sometimes peek in their windows at night. They just gave up. Now the town is mine!"

"I still don't know what a human is…" she reiterated.

"You said you lived on a farm, right?" he asked.

"Well, yes, of course, my whole life was spent on a farm. Well, until now."

"Well, you probably had someone there that lived in a house and fed you every morning, maybe rode around on a tractor?"

"Yes! The Farmer! Of course!" She excitedly recalls.

"Well, that Farmer is a human. With the two legs and the walking upright, wearing clothes for some reason."

"I…I had no idea…" she says as though she genuinely knew nothing about anything.

"It's okay girl. Not your fault. You've been sheltered. I understand. But let me show you something else that's going to totally blow your mind."

Chupacabra led the cow into a slightly smaller building than The Old Red Barn. He told her it was something called a Market. As soon as he followed him inside, she froze. It wasn't like being frozen in the river, but more like frozen in shock. She couldn't believe what she was seeing. There was food in every direction. Apples, oranges, greens, reds, and every vibrant color imaginable.

"Here, try one of these. The humans call them Bananas or something."

She took a bite and fell into a blissful state of uncertainty. She felt as though her life had just started. Who was this wonderful yet frightening creature the universe had placed into her life? She looked at him and simply said, "Thank you!"

"Thank me for what? Not eating you?" he jokingly asked.

"Well, that too, but thank you for saving men. Thank you for showing me all of this," she spoke with a large tear welling up in her eye.

"No problem, girl. I don't get along with too many others, but I'm enjoying the company."

From that point on, every time the cow and the Chupacabra looked at each other, it grew more endearing. Eventually, it reached the point where neither wanted to live without the other. The humans never returned, and they spent years building a life together. They fell deeply in love, never caring about their physical differences, never looking back to the lives they lived before that fateful day at the river. When the food ran out, he scavenged for more. When intruders poked their noses around, he'd scare them off. She kept the town in working order. She never realized how much she learned from watching The Farmer back home. Together, they were just simply happy.

Now, they say that miracles happen on a daily basis; we just need to pay more attention to witness every one of them. And though nature has a strict set of rules, sometimes love can overpower those rules and create those miracles. We're not sure of the day or even the month, nor do we even know the real name or location of this small town they called home. But whenever it was and wherever it was, such a miracle took place. The Chupacabra and the cow brought the third member of their family into the world.

He began to walk immediately, learned to feed from his mother's utters, and even grazed in the field within days. He was adventurous and rambunctious, always running around the town, knocking things over and leaving a disaster area behind him. You think the wind outside is making a mess.

You should've seen this calf. He looked exactly like his mother and nothing at all like his father. His father would joke, 'Good thing he looks like you. I wouldn't wish my ugliness on anyone!' But inside, he had the beating heart of a wild Chupacabra, and that's the part of his father he was proud to possess!"

In the audience, Chupacabra Cow felt proud. He could feel the Chupacabra blood shooting through with arteries like lava. Chake continued the story.

"One day, while Chupacabra Dad was miles from town gathering food, Mom Cow was fixing up a fence that the kid had knocked over while chasing a rabbit. Meanwhile, the baby cow wandered into the house they'd made their home and curled up into a ball on the carpeted floors. He was quickly woken up by a loud "Moo!" from his mother, followed by a crashing thud. He quickly ran to the window to see a group of humans celebrating in the middle of the street after tipping his mother over.

She struggled to her feet, looking towards the house, and screamed, "Stay inside! Hide!" He wanted to help, so he headed toward the door. "No! Don't come out here! Hide Son!"

He looked back out the window as they pushed her again, and she fell flat on her side. Again, she struggled to her feet and tried to escape, but at this point, she was hurt and unable to run. The humans were laughing and celebrating as they tipped her over another time. This time, she didn't attempt to get back to her feet. She didn't move.

She was gone.

"Mom?"

The humans looted the small town. There wasn't much to take, and what they didn't take, they just destroyed.

It was dark now. The Chupacabra Cow hadn't moved from the window. He just stared at his mom, hoping she would just stand up, but she didn't. The humans lit a huge fire in the center of town, pulling boards off buildings to keep it lit. After a while, they began to light loose boards on fire and toss them into the abandoned houses and shops.

Building by building, he watched his entire world burn to the ground. The smoke in the air filled his lungs, and his eyes were stained with tears. He hid in darkness for what seemed like an eternity.

"Nooooo!" A howl filled the night. He knew his father had returned but had never heard him make a sound so chilling and full of grief.

He stared back out the window to see him standing by his mother's body. The humans staggered towards him, armed with wooden planks and old rusty farming equipment.

"No, Dad!" he yelled and ran out of the house.

"Get back into the house now..." he said in the most sinister voice he's ever imagined could come from his own father's growling salivated mouth. "NOW!" he ordered!

"Please don't hurt my father! Please don't hurt my father!" he muttered again and again. He could hear what sounded like violent chaos taking place just outside of the house he was hiding in. He buried his head in blankets and covered his ears. He just knew that any second, the humans would bust through the door.

But moments later...

"Son... It's okay... You're safe."

"Dad!" He uncovered his head to see a shadowy silhouette of his father standing at the door with the fire burning behind him. As he walked closer, he could see that his father was drenched in blood. "Dad, are you okay.?" he cried.

"I'm fine, son. I'm fine. We have to go now."

"But what about the humans?"

"You don't need to worry about them anymore, son. Come on, we have to go right now." Father and son walked into the night with only each other and the stars to light the way.

"Where are we going, Dad?" The calf wondered.

"Your mother told me of a place. A place where you can have a wonderful life, where you'll be safe and happy."

"You mean a place where WE'LL be safe and happy, right?" His dad looked at the passing dirt under his steps,

"Son... it's a tough world out here. Some call me the most ferocious creature in the wild, and I was barely surviving until I met your mom. I don't want you to live that kind of life. You deserve more than I could ever support you out here. The town is gone, kid, your mother... she's gone too..."

"But Dad! I can be tough like you."

"I know you can. You've got my heart and Chupacabra blood running in your veins. You're going to be just fine. And so will I. Someday, you'll going to do something special. I'll be checking in on you, kid."

A full day later, they approached a large, beautiful farm with a huge population of every kind of animal.

"This is it, kid."

"Dad, I don't want you to go." His dad obviously didn't want to leave his son either. But after losing his love and not being able to protect her, he felt as though this was the only choice.

"Go...!"

Cow hung his head low. He looked back at the toughest creature in the world, fighting back the tears. He, too, fought not to cry. If this was the last time his father was to see him, he wanted to be strong. He heard his father say, "I love you, son," and watched him disappear into the thick brush on the other side of the dirt road. The cow was seen by a Farmer on the Farm. He quickly ran out and opened the gate, looking a bit confused, but was welcomed into the Farm and into a whole new life. Years passed, and day-to-day farm life dwindled the cow's memories of the small town, even his mother and father. He was so young back then. Sometimes, we all lose memories to the ticking clock. You might think it's to make room for new ones. But other times, those memories can come back to life. Because that Farm was THIS farm, and that incredible half cow half Chupacabra is right here in this very Barn."

The crowd's hearts collectively skipped a beat. All the other cows looked at each other as if they'd just met.

"Well, who is it?" asked an elder hen.

"He's right here! Let me introduce to you CHUPACABRA COW!"

Everyone stared at him in awe. He finally got the reactions and the attention he's always wanted, and now he has no idea what to do with it. He smiled awkwardly with a big toothy grin.

"Um, Hey, everybody!"

You mean that story you were telling on the wagon earlier was real?" Cow nervously replied, "Yeah, I guess so. Uh, yeah."

From that moment on, he was no longer just an average everyday ordinary cow. All he needed was someone to believe in him, and now he's learning how to believe in himself.

After hours of answering questions he didn't know the answers to, Chicken Snake finally broke up what seemed like a breaking news press conference.

"Okay, everyone! It's getting late! The Chupacabra Cow will be here in the morning and every morning. Plenty of time to mob him with questions later. Go to your stables and pens, get some sleep!" Everyone wandered off in different directions, still buzzing from the fantastic jaw-dropping story of Chupacabra Cow; Chake pulled him into a dark corner of the Barn out of range of any listening ears. "CC..." he said.

"CC?" Asked Chupacabra Cow.

"Yeah, I'm going to call you CC. I mean, Chupacabra Cow has, like, 5 syllables, and I almost say it wrong every time. So, you call me Chake & I'll you CC!"

He smiled. CC looked at him with a blank face, struggling with a thousand questions, all trying to come out at the same time.

"That story... Where? Who? How did you?" CC stumbled.

"Did you like it?" Chake confidently asked.

"It was amazing, but... How? Is that what really happened to me? How do you know this stuff? Where did you?"

"Calm down, calm down! Did you see the crowd? Did you see how that reacted? Isn't that what you wanted?"

"Well, yeah, sure, but I..." "But what? You told everyone earlier that you were half Chupacabra and half cow. Right?" Chake sternly asked.

"Right..." Cow confirms. "Well, I just filled in the blanks. It's storytelling. Everyone here needs a good story. It's all they really have to look forward to. For the longest time, I was the only one telling stories, and after a while, to be honest, I couldn't stand telling the same story again and again. Then you came along with an equally incredible story, and I thought to myself, 'PERFECT!' Maybe you could take some of the pressure off of me to tell my story constantly. So now you have your own story to tell!" Chake was pleased with this idea and looked forward to not being the only celebrity on The Farm. "But is the story true? How did you know?" asked CC.

"CC, I read the same flying trash papers that you do. I read the story about the Chupacabra weeks ago. And do you really believe every single word of MY story?"

"Well, of course, it's the greatest story ever told. Everyone believes it." CC muttered, feeling like he was about to learn something mind-blowing.

"Look, honestly, between you and me. There's only one goat that saw the entire thing. He found my egg and another egg lying near the fence. He told me that the crows did indeed fly off with the other one and that we were found inside of a snake's belly. When I hatched, I was half chicken and half snake? That's really all that I know. I made up the rest. Like I said, I filled in the blanks, just like with your story. You said that you're a Chupacabra Cow. Well, I took stuff from the trash papers, used a little imagination, and filled in the missing parts."

Chake looked very pleased with himself. As he should be. His story and CC's story entertained the entire farm for years. Without his story, there would be nothing to distract the average farm animal from its daily routine. He knew he was offering a service and acting out his purpose on the farm.

"So, what do I do now?" CC asked.

"You learn your own story. Remember every word. Because as soon as the sun rises, everyone's going to want to hear it again and again and again. It took me a while to recall everything. Once in a while, I'll add something new to change it up a bit, but they'll love it. And don't be afraid. Never show any fear. Remember, you've got the spirit of a wild Chupacabra. Nothing can stand in your way."

"Goodnight, CC. Tomorrow is a brand new day!"

Chake returned to the chicken house, and CC lay down right where he stood. He struggled to remember every aspect of his own new story, but after such a long, exhausting, yet exciting day, sleep came out of nowhere.

The Old Red Barn fell quiet.

CHAPTER 4
Who Did This?

A few hours into sleep, "CRASH!" A loud, shattering sound woke everyone in the barn. CC slowly opened his eyes with a wide yawn and shuffled around the hay he slept on. He noticed the raindrops had stopped hitting the steel roof, but it was still a tad windy as a breeze shot over him from a crack in the nearby window.

He was tired, really tired. It seemed as though he didn't sleep a wink. He closed his eyes, but the bright glowing orange light made him think it was morning, so he yawned again and stood up. He composed himself and said aloud, "Tired or not, today I'm a new cow! I'm going to tell my story and set the world on…FIRE!!!"

Cow noticed the entire corner of the Barn was engulfed in flames.

"Everyone out! Get out! The barn's on fire! Everybody Run!"

The creaky barn doors burst open, and everyone inside ran for their lives. Chake & CC stood by the gates and gave the now half-burnt barn one last look to ensure everyone had made it out.

But they didn't.

The other cows, the only family he'd ever known, were trapped as a fiery beam from the ceiling fell, blocking their path to the gate. Chake quickly left the barn and returned with a bucket filled with rainwater; he handed it to CC, who then doused the beams, putting that particular fire out. The cows pushed from the other side, and CC pulled from his side until the beams broke into ashy pieces. More beams continued falling from above. Everything inside was covered in flames. CC, Chake, and the other cows finally made it out before the Barn collapsed. By the time everyone made it safely to the field, The Old Red Barn was gone.

"Our home…" someone said sadly and softly. Just then, the Farmer walked out of his front door. His house was only a hundred years away. He looked towards The Old Red Barn and stared at an inferno that had already spread to the nearby grain silo. The smell of burning grain and the old wood was actually very pleasant, but that was the only silver lining.

Within another 30 minutes, the entire barn was reduced to a large black pile of ash. Without that impressive landmark, the farm looked small and empty as the morning sun rose. The windmill survived, and the Farmer's house was spared, but it was the Barn that defined that place; it made it home. Now they all stood in a muddy field with nothing but hallow hearts and questions. The Farmer just stood there for a moment, placed his hands over his face, adjusted his hat, and went back inside the house. That Barn has been in his family for generations. Sure, the residents of the farm community lost a home, but he lost a legacy.

"Thank you for saving us," one of the cows said to CC.

"Yeah, if it weren't for you and Chicken Snake, we'd be part of that pile of ash over there." said another.

"I'm just glad everyone made it out," CC said in a relieved tone. Chake walked up to the cows.

"All of my best ties were in there," he said as he adjusted the one he was wearing. "I only have this one I have on, and this other one I managed to grab on the way out. It's huge. I had planned on making a bunch of smaller ties out of it, but I think I have a better idea." Chake wrapped the tie around CC's neck and tied a perfect Full Windsor knot. "If you're going to be a celebrity, you better dress the part. You saved us all, kid. You deserve it."

CC's lips quivered a bit, momentarily forgetting that his home just burned to the ground. "I don't know what to say, Chake…"

Chake quickly replied, "You know exactly what to say, CC. You just need to learn how to say it."

CC felt so many things at once. Sadness over the loss of the Barn, Pride for his new friendship with Chake, and his part in evacuating the barn. He also felt sorry for all those who had been displaced by the fire. The Farmer and his dogs began herding everyone into different fields, some rather far away. This community had always been close, always within range of each other. Sometimes, there would be a small fence between different types, but we'd always be within talking range. The pigs lost their pen inside the barn and were the first of us to be led away to a new home. One by one, they disappeared down a long rocky trail and into a fenced-in area by the pond on the edge of the farm. "Did anyone notice that the pigs were already outside when we escaped from the barn?" asked a sheep.

He continued. "Rumor has it that they were all about to be shipped to The Great Farm. At first, they were happy to go, but some crows came along and told them that pigs don't go to The Great Farm. Instead, they go to a terrible place where they become something called Bacon."

"Oh, come on. You know those crows are always starting awful rumors." Chake responded.

Sheep continued. "But think about it: who else would have a reason to burn down the barn. The pigs never really got along with The Farmer. They always complain about the food, about not having enough room in the pen."

"Well, what about the crows themselves?" said a mouse. "I've seen them destroy The Farmer's crops. They've never liked any of us. There's a reason he put those scarecrows out in the fields. I mean, they're called SCARECROWS! They have a motive. They could've set the fire and then flew away undetected."

Suddenly, a crow swoops down from the sky, "I heard everything you just said, you little twit. I should take you back to the fields and serve you for breakfast!"

Chase stepped in front of the mouse and had a brief stare-down with the crow. He never liked crows since learning they stole the egg right next to his own.

"No one is having anyone for breakfast," he said. The crow began laughing. For some reason, the crows would always laugh at Chicken Snake. It never seemed as though they were laughing AT him but laughing because they knew something he didn't.

"Well, Mr. Half and Half, maybe you should ask that tasty little mouse over there what HE was doing when the fire started. I happened to notice new mouse traps all over The Farm. And I also noticed they've been working quite well. So, if anyone has a reason to burn down your home with everyone in it, maybe it's the rat!" he cunningly said and then flew away.

"What about the sheep! They hate being sheered! I heard that one say he wanted to get even with The Farmer!"

An out-of-sight voice said, "How about the egg-laying chickens? Stuck in a small room all day, forced to lay eggs. Then The farmer steals their eggs and never brings them back! Plus, the henhouse is outside of the barn. Maybe they did it!"

Said another voice with a theory, "The Horses have always said the barn took up too much of their space. Maybe they burned it down to get more room for stables and running space!"

"It was the Farmer's Dogs! They're always making threats and talking down to us!"

The accusations just kept flying in from all directions. After a few minutes, hearing any particular voice over the cluttering arguments became impossible.

"SHUT UP!" yelled Chake. "Listen to yourselves! This isn't making anything any easier! Look, I know we're all extremely upset. We've lost everything we had in there. I lost all of my good ties, all of my trash papers, everything. But you must realize that we're all very lucky to have gotten out alive, and the only thing we have left is each other."

Chake took charge and began pacing the field in front of each group of animals as if he were the Brigadier General of a military battalion.

"We have to keep a clear view of the facts here. Yes, the barn has burnt down. Yes, there has to be a reason why the barn burned down. And yes, there's a very good chance that it was burned down by somebody standing in this muddy field." CC watched as his friend commanded the situation. He was respected by everyone on The Farm, so assuming a leadership role during such a tragedy was expected and accepted.

"Over the next few days, I will conduct a proper, honest, and fair investigation. I will make a list of possible suspects and one by one, I will do my very best to either develop an alibi and scratch them off the list or deliver evidence that proves beyond a shadow of a doubt they were the guilty party that burned down our home. Once the Farmer figures out where everyone is going, I will begin my investigation. Until then, there will be no more fighting, no more arguing, and no more accusations. Do you all understand me?" Chake asked as he scanned everyone before him, and they all affirmed.

Throughout the rest of that day, The Farmer divided this once closer-knit community into different fields and areas throughout the farmlands. The horse still had their stables, and the chickens still had their hen house and fenced-in area, and that's where Chake would map out his strategy for the detective work that would undoubtedly consume him for several days and weeks to come. CC and the rest of the cows remained where they were. Luckily, that muddy field they escaped to was the same field they usually grazed. Even luckier, it was right next to the chicken coup. The sheep were led away to a field out of sight, where they shared space with the goats. And everyone else, the bugs, the mice, the cats and owls, they all just kind of scattered throughout the area looking for something that even resembled shelter.

Later that afternoon, "CC!" whispered Chake through the fence separating the cows and chickens.

"I'm here, Chake."

"Good, I've spent the past few hours compiling a list of possible suspects. I have to say it's a little longer and a lot more detailed than I had first assumed it would be." Chake said while stressfully looking up and down his list. "I can't do this alone, CC. I need someone with me as we question and interrogate. I need someone brave and respected, someone I can trust." Chake said while staring directly at CC.

"Well, Ed the horse has a lot of respect, maybe Chuckles the Cat. He can move around the farm with ease, and those scary claws might come in handy," said CC while pondering other options.

"No... what? Do you have fertilizer for brains? I'm talking about you!" Chake laughed out.

"Me? Well, I don't know the first thing about detective work. Also, I'm a little too big to be hopping over all of these fences." CC explained.

"Do you think I know what I'm doing? I've never tried to solve a crime before." Chake revealed. "It's just like our stories. We know what we have to do, so let's just fill in the blanks. We'll learn as we go. As long as it LOOKS like we know what we're doing, everyone will believe that we do."

Chake went on confidently. "You and I are the only two that are even slightly qualified to figure this out. We have to at least attempt to find out who burned our home to the ground and bring them to justice. Otherwise, it'll be an unanswered question we'll take with us to The Great Farm and beyond. Chicken Snake & Chupacabra Cow, CC and Chake, Farm detectives! Time's already wasting away. Let's solve this crime!" rallied Chake.

CC thought for a brief moment, looked at the other cows lazily grazing, and looked at the ash blowing in the breeze from the once beautiful and sheltering Old Red Barn. Looking back at Chake, he said, "Yeah, let's solve this crime."

Chake began to go over the plan, "Okay, it seems as though The Farmer has finally settled everyone into their new homes, and they're scattered rather far across the farmlands. I sketched a map and traced a route best for our time and effort. The Farmer put the pigs by the pond, the sheep and goats are in the western grassy area, the crows normally hang out in the cornfields, and the cows will be easy because they're right here…"

"Wait…" CC interrupts, you're questioning the other cows?"

"We have to question everyone, CC. The chickens are also on this list. We can't leave a single stone unturned. My research has revealed that just about everyone here has a motive. Everyone here has a gripe with The Farmer. It's only fair that we include everyone and question everything, even if its awkward to do so."

CC understood, and Chake went on with the investigation's plan.

"Since we're right here, we'll start with the chickens. I've already told all of them to gather behind the henhouse in 15 minutes. I'll ask the questions, you take mental notes, then we'll meet up afterward and discuss whether they're to stay on the list of possible suspects or scratched off the list if their alibi checks out. Oh, and don't worry about hopping fences. I'm not only a fantastic storyteller but also a master-level lock picker. These talons have gotten me in every area on the farm, including inside The Farmer's house. But that's a story for another time."

"Wow, where did you learn all of this?" CC asked in awe.

"Well, being a farm celebrity has its perks, kid. When I was first hatched, The Farmer knew he had a novelty in me. Originally, he would keep me inside his house in a comfy little coup. Other humans would stop by and bask in my glory! Haha… I'm kidding, but they would certainly be amazed at a half chicken half-snake combo. But at night, The Farmer would always fall asleep on the couch watching something called a TV. For hours every night, he'd watch detective shows and mystery movies. Honestly, I've waited my entire life for a crime to solve, and THAT, my boy, is why I'm ready." Chake said proudly and eagerly. Chake opened the gate between the cows and the chickens and led CC behind the henhouse, where every chicken, hen, and rooster waited. The investigation was underway.

CHAPTER 5
Law, Order, and Chickens

The chickens were gathered around and ready. CC stood behind Chake, ready to take notes. Everyone was still damp and muddy from last night's happening.

"Okay, my fellow chickens, I would hate to think that we lost the barn due to the actions of one of my own, but we cannot eliminate any possibilities until we find out who did this," Chake said sternly.

"But Chake... why, why would you even think it could possibly be one of us?" asked a concerned chicken named Lionel.

"Lionel, I would be heartbroken if it were a fellow member of the poultry community, but as painful as it is to say this, the chickens have a motive." Chake regretfully said as he kicked some loose gravel by his talons.

"What's a motive?" Asked Otis Chicken. "Yeah, a motive? Is that like some kind of new song?" Asked Daryl Chicken. "Hey, everyone! Chicken Snake is about to sing us a song!" The crowd of chickens all got excited and moved in ever closer.

"No, it's not a song, and no, I'm not about to sing anything. Stay focused, chickens! A Motive is a reason to do something. Something like burning down the barn. THAT it was a motive is."

"Wait, what motive could possibly have to do such a thing?" Gilmore Chicken asked. "None of us would ever do something like that!"

"Well, Gilmore, then you and the rest of us have nothing to worry about, right?" confirmed Chake.

"Of course, we have nothing to worry about, Chake!" added Roger Chicken. "We're just simple chickens. We have no gripes or issues."

"Well, that is not entirely true," said Chake. "For how many years has The Farmer forced the egg layers into the henhouse, held them in tiny cages, and forced them to lay eggs for days at a time, and then he's taken those eggs as soon as they arrived, never to be seen again.

Generations of our baby chicks stolen before they could even hatch. How many years have each of us watched as he grabbed them and placed them inside cartons that looked to be specially made to hold our eggs?"

"But we've always believed they were taken to The Great Farm to be hatched and live better lives than we could provide for them here," another chicken named Ronald says gleefully.

"That's a nice story, it really is, but have we already forgotten about the trash paper we found about a year ago?" Chake boldly mentioned. The crowd hushed, and they began to hang their heads and appeared to be deep in a fearful thought.

"We all saw those images. I know most of us have chosen to bury and forget it, but you cannot deny that we saw what we saw."

"Maybe it was just a scary story. It was make-believe." bawked out Chantal Chicken. "The humans sell those eggs as food. Okay? None of us want to believe it, but it's true. And can't we not just simply forget the headline BUFFALO CHICKEN WINGS $4.99 A POUND? There were pictures right beneath it. The humans are also dipping our wings in buffalo blood and selling them as well! You can't deny this! Sure, stories of The Great Farm make you feel better; they make you work harder and feel as though there's a reward waiting for you after your time is up here at The Farm, but we all know what really happens. So yes, even though it's our home, we all have every reason to burn this place to the ground."

"But we didn't, Chake," Chantal said with a quivering beak.

"Well, let's make sure we can prove that without a single doubt," said Chake before he turned to CC. "Did you make a list of all the motives I just mentioned?"

"Yeah, Chake, but…" CC hesitated. "Are you saying that The Great Farm isn't real?"

"I don't know, CC. No one knows until you get on that big truck and find out for yourself. But we can't get sidetracked. There's far too much work to be done. Follow me CC."

One by one, chicken by chicken, Chake asked each of them where they were last night when the fire broke out. Each of them basically said the exact same thing. "I was right next to you, Chake!"

Chake marked each one of them off the list, one after another until he got to the very last chicken. Vinnie was standing in the background for the entire questioning process. While Chake was the celebrity chicken everyone clamored around, Vinnie Chicken was the oldest, the wisest, and the chicken everyone respected as the leader of the coup. "Chake, we all understand what needs to be done here, and we all respect you for taking on such a task. It was a tragic night, and while we still have our outside henhouse and field, we lost our favorite place within that barn. Yes, I agree that we should all face the truth when it comes to The Great Farm. We must all agree to stop lying to ourselves about what we saw in that terrible trash paper. But I believe your investigation with your chicken brothers and sisters has come to an end, and the verdict here is not guilty."

Chake knew Vinnie was right, "I agree, boss. CC, mark the chickens off the list. We were all together when the fire broke out. The proof was seen with my own two eyes." CC followed the order, "Chickens are off the list, boss!"

"Might I make a suggestion, son," Vinnie added. "Maybe think of those who gave no value to the lives of us that were inside the burning barn. Consider those who live elsewhere and have nothing to lose. You might find some answers from those who've looked down on this farm society since there has been a farm society."

Chake fell into thinking mode. "The Farmer's Dogs…" he said with a flash. "Those dogs have harassed us and threatened us for as long as I can remember. They're the entire reason The Farmer had to move me from inside the house all those years ago. The barking, the insults, the growling, the evil intentions."

Chake began to boil while thinking of the tenant his fellow farm residents endured. He grabbed the notebook and underlined boldly THE FARMER'S DOGS! "Is that where we're heading next, Chake?" asked CC.

"Not quite yet. We're going to have to prepare ourselves a little more before tackling that part of the case. I have a long history with those mutts. The part of my story where my mother pranked Dale the dog. That wasn't made up. That actually happened, and rumor has it that he's still alive and living inside the house."

Chake went on. "There's a funny thing about history. Stories are often told to benefit the ones who are telling the story. I've heard that when the dogs speak of the incident, it's not nearly the same story I would talk about my mom."

"What do you mean? The dogs can make up stories as well?" CC asked.

"Not as good as we can by any means, but when they tell the story, they conveniently leave out the years of awful behavior they've shown to those on the farm. They always seem to omit the parts where they chase the animals into pens and nip at their heels. They forget to add the constant threats of hopping the fences and tearing them apart with their teeth. Yeah, we need to prepare for the dogs." Chake looked as though he was already strategizing, "So who's next?" CC broke up Chake's train of thought.

"Well, that's easy. Let's head back through that gate, and we'll be there," Chake instructed. "Oh, it's OUR turn."

CC wasn't too excited about throwing accusations at his own family of cows. Still, after seeing Chake take on the chickens, he knew it had to be done. CC and Chake creaked open the old fence separating the cows and chickens, lightly shut it behind them, made sure it latched, and wandered back onto the muddy field where everyone he grew up knowing was lying in wait.

CHAPTER 6
A Cow Spiracy

"Don't get us wrong, Chicken Snake and Chupacabra Cow," yelled Cow before they were even in place to start the questioning. "We are HUGE fans of both of your stories. Last night, you know, before the fire, was one of the most intense and life-changing nights we cows have ever had. To think we had such a magnificent member of the cow family right next to us for all these years. It's just incredible! But we overheard every single word you said to the chickens. If you're coming over here to accuse us cows of anything having to do with the loss of our beloved barn, you guys can just keep walking."

Chake attempted to calm them down but was immediately cut off by CC.

"Cows, I've known you my entire life. Whether or not we come from the same bloodlines, we're still family. We're not here to accuse you or anything. We just need to gather facts.

"I literally just watched Chicken Snake question his entire coup. He pointed out reasons they might have had cause to do this, and, one by one, he cleared them all. So please, for the sake of this investigation and out of respect to me, your fellow cow. Just answer these questions, cooperate, and it'll be over before you know it."

The cows looked at each other while standing in their grazing field and, without a word, came to the same reply,

"Nope..." they all said at once and began to walk away.

"HEY! YOU LISTEN TO ME RIGHT NOW COWS!" CC hollered out as if it were one of the first times he'd heard his own voice gain such inflection. Even Chake flinched and took a step backward. "You're not dealing with the old Cow any longer! Sure, I may look pretty much exactly like all of you. Still, inside, I had the heart of a wild Chupacabra. While the cow in me would let you put me down and disrespect me, the Chupacabra inside doesn't take crap for anyone."

The cows immediately stepped back into the group, giving CC their full attention.

"Now you're going to answer these questions, you're going to pay attention, and you're going to respect Chake and me like you've never respected anyone in your life! UNDERSTAND?" CC scolded.

"Dude, nice…" Chake whispered behind him.

"The floor is yours, Chake." CC motioned for Chake to step up and get it started.

"Well, now that we have your attention. Thanks, CC." CC moved to his planter perch as a note taker behind Chake, who took a deep breath and jumped into it. "Since you heard what I said to the chickens, you know exactly what I'm trying to figure out. That heaping pile of smoldering dust over there was our home. Take a look at it; all the memories we've all created, everything we owned inside, are lying right there."

The cows, including CC, all stared at what was left of The Old Red Barn, which now resembled the large fire pit on the other side of the fence by the dirt road where The Farmer burned leaves.

"Now we're not here to accuse anyone, we're not here to cast blame without evidence, we're simply going to make sure that all of you are one hundred percent innocent." Chake looked over his notes, "Okay, let's talk motives…" he continued.

"Why are we talking about motives? We barely made it out alive ourselves. If it wasn't for the two of you, we'd all be in that pile of ash," said Cow.

"That's true, but…" CC chimed in. "When I kicked open the barn doors, I noticed one of you was already outside," CC revealed. "Yeah, it's all coming back to me. The Barn doors were unlatched, and I remember seeing one of you off in the distance, covered in windy darkness. I didn't get a clear picture of who it was and didn't think too much of it at the time because of all the chaos going on, but yeah, one of you was definitely outside before the fire was started."

"Well, we'll ask once. If no one steps forward and admits to being the one standing in the field when we're escaping, then we'll have to adapt slightly more intense procedures." Chake commanded before giving them to the count of five to reveal who it was.

"5… 4… 3…" the cows began to look amongst themselves frantically."

CC paused the count with further intimidation, "You're talking to half a snake and half Chupacabra. If we put those halves together, we'll easily get you to talk!" Chake continued counting, "2...1..."

"Okay, okay, geez, everyone, it was me, okay? It was me..."

Cow stepped forward. CC and the particular cow had always gotten along quite well, so it surprised him that HE was now the main suspect.

"Okay, Cow, please explain to everyone here why you were already outside in the field while the rest of us barely escaped the fire."

"Yes, I was out here, but it's not because I'm guilty of starting any fires or anything close to that, it's just... I... well... it's...it's quite embarrassing."

"Well, right now, you're the prime suspect of a crime that costs all of us our homes," said Chake, clarifying the point. "So, let's hear your alibi, or it's looking like we're about to close this case."

"Fine, fine... It was the bad wheat!"

Everyone looked puzzled.

"Bad wheat?" CC asked.

Cow explained, "Yeah, the bad wheat from last week. I know it was rotten, I knew we weren't supposed to touch it, but I slept through dinner that day, and, well, I was starving later on, and..."

Chake cut him off.

"You knew we were investigating the burning of the barn, right? No one cares if you ate some spoiled wheat."

"Well, my stomach cared. It cared a lot." Cow replied. "Ever since I saw how the other cows were making fun of him," motioning to CC, "There was no way I was going to let them know what I was going through."

"What are you talking about, Cow?" CC asked. "The only thing you did was pass a little gas that night. My stomach had me exploding over here. I can't keep anything in me for more than a few minutes. They laughed at you and called you The Amazing Farting Cow."

"Yeah, let's not bring that up. I'm the... the Chupacabra guy now, so, yeah, so, old news..." CC muttered.

Cow continued, "So last night, it was still really bad. At some point, I just couldn't hold it anymore. So, I unlatched the barn doors and took care of my business away from all of you. I knew if you heard or saw me drop that big stinking...."

"Okay! We get it!" Chake cut him off before it got too graphic.

"I was just being respectful to the rest of the herd. I was out there for a while. If you need the evidence, I'm sure there's plenty still against the fence line over in that direction."

Chake wanted to throw up a little but regained his composure.

"No, that's... that's fine..."

Cow continued, "It was sure windy and rainy, but I'd rather be out in the weather than be known as The Incredible Crapping Cow or something."

"That's understandable," said Chake. "I saw the barn doors slam open and everyone running out. Moments later, the entire barn was burning down. So, if I'm guilty of anything, it's having a bad cow belly."

"Cross him and all the cows off the list, CC. This investigation is still wide open."

"So, while you were out here, did you happen to see anyone else wandering around?" Chake asked.

"The only ones I saw outside were The Farmer and one of his dogs. But that was hours before the fire. It was really storming out. I could barely stand. They were just out latching shutters and tying things down so they didn't blow away. After that, he just went back into the house." Cow recalled.

"And the dog that was with him?"

"I didn't see where he went. I certainly didn't go looking for him. One of them bit my tail when it accidentally poked through their fence a couple of days ago. Then he said that he's now got a taste for cow's blood, so I don't want to be anywhere near The Farmer's dogs."

He shuddered. "Well, if we're all finished here, I really need to, um, take care of a little more business, uh, as far away from here as I can get." Cow said while obviously straining to hold back something we really don't care to describe. "Gotta go!" he said as he ran off quickly.

While the cows dispersed, Chake was again solely focused on his thoughts. CC broke the silence.

"So cows scratch, and chickens scratch."

"Haha, you said chicken scratch..." Chake mocked.

"Why's that funny? CC inquired.

"It's a thing that is said when... the humans... oh, never mind... it's not important." He takes another brief pause. "What IS important is that we head over to the front yard of The Farmer's house where the dogs are. We'll have to be careful, but I have a strange feeling we're about to slam the lid down on this case."

Before CC and Chake braved the lair of the dogs, they suited up. CC flung an old tire around his neck and grabbed a rusty rake that had been sitting against a tree for years. Chake found a small garden shovel and wrapped himself up in old rags that were lying around the field. Chake dipped his wing in the mud, smeared it across his face, darkening his eyes, and then repeated the warpaint onto Chupacabra Cow. They were ready for the dogs; they were ready for war.

CHAPTER 7
Not Letting Sleeping Dogs Lie

Neither Chake nor CC said a word as they opened and closed fence after fence heading towards the lair of the Farmer's dogs. The quiet clang of each latch carefully being passed through rattled more nerves. Every crunch of Earth under their feet solidified their determination. Chake thought of his mother and what these very dogs put her and the rest of the chickens through. CC thought of the story he had just heard from Cow about how one of these dogs nipped at his tail.

The sky began to color itself darker as evening claimed its rightful place. Just 20 years away, the dog known as Luke caught a glimpse and began his roaring bark routine. This alerted the other dogs, who growled out their canine symphony. They ran to the edge of the fence, nosed pressed through the chain link, salivating as the intruders drew near. Their barking was deafening and terrifying, but neither took a step backward.

"SHUT UP!" Chake roared as he smacked the fence with his weaponized shovel, grazing Luke across the nose.

"Arrr, arrr, arrr!" Luke's threatening demeanor instantly changed to a cowering yelp.

"You've got a lot of nerve coming even close to our yard, Chicken Snake. You and whoever your cow friend is are about to learn a painful lesson in messing with us dogs," said the dog known as Garrett. "We know you're the son of a chicken that once attacked us in our own yard. It's time for revenge. We never forget."

"And that's exactly why we're here, you smelly mutt!" fired back Chake. "You dogs have made life miserable for every other animal on this farm for as long as anyone can remember. My mom just got a small measure of payback, and I'm proud to be her son."

"You're nothing but a freak covered in feathers and scales," Garrett Dog insulted. "You act so brave on the other side of that fence, but I

46

dare you to take one step through that gate. I promise you'll never leave this yard alive."

Just then, CC kicked open the gate, walked into the yard, and got face-to-face with Garrett Dog. "You were saying?"

Garrett Dog backed down briefly but at once found his spine as the four other dogs began to surround CC. Chake flapped and perched on the fence.

"CC, get out of there!" Chake pleaded.

"Luke, Syd, Billy, Fred… You all pick a leg to tear off, and I'll choke him with his own stupid tie," Garrett ordered.

Luke lunged at one of CC's back legs and received a solid kick across his mouth, sending him back into the fence. Syd jumped fangs first at the other rear leg and was met with the same fate. Billy tried to attack CC as well but found himself on the other end of a powerful head butt that put his lights out. Fred looked at the carnage instantly put out onto his fellow dogs by this angry 1500lb cow and quickly decided it was in his best interest to sit this one out.

"I'm cool… I'm cool…" he said.

CC was breathing fire at this point and turned his attention back to Garrett Dog, "You were saying?" He repeated but in a thicker, angrier tone.

"Look, we don't want any trouble Cow. Let's leave the past behind us, okay?"

Chake butted in. "Now that we've come to an agreement let's talk about why we're here."

Chake flapped over and landed on top of the dog's house, symbolically standing before the dogs like an occupying force.

"We have a few questions," he stated.

"Wait a minute, Chake. Before we start this part of the investigation, I have something to say." All the dogs recovered and staggered before CC. "For years, this yard and the dog in it have been a source of constant fear for the entire farm. You've chased us, threatened us, even bit us. Well, that all ends right here and right now!" CC demanded.

"We were just doing what The Farmer told us to do. It's our job to keep order and to make sure everyone gets to where The Farmer needed them to be," answered Garrett Dog.

"There's keeping order and doing your job, and then there's being awful, terrible jerks. You can do your job and be nice, and you WILL do your job, and you WILL be nice from this point on." Ordered CC. "Okay, I get it. You've got a deal. We'll be…nice."

The dogs all agreed.

"If I even hear a peep about ANYONE getting harassed by The Farmer's Dogs ever again, I will come back with every cow, horse, pig, and sheep, and we'll stampede this yard and everyone in it into the ground. Understand?" threatened CC.

"Yeah, yeah, we totally understand." The dogs hung their heads low and agreed.

"Well, alright, let's get started," said Chake. The dogs gave Chake their undivided attention while CC stood beside him in almost a secretary/bodyguard role.

"As you know, The Old Red Barn is gone. Last night, someone or something burned our home to the ground." Chake began. "We are conducting an investigation. We're questioning everyone from our closest friends to our worst enemies until we find out who did this."

"Wait. You think that we had something to do with the barn fire?" Billy Dog asked.

"We are here to figure out where you were last night. Then we'll decide whether or not you're guilty or innocent. We know at least one of you was roaming around with The Farmer last night. So, you're going to tell us where you were and who was patrolling the farm."

"Well, I was out with The Farmer last night during the storm. We were securing the farm, making sure all of you were inside the barn," said Fred Dog. "But the winds were strong, and after locking the place down, we headed inside the house."

"Where were the rest of you?" asked Chake.

"To be honest, Chicken Snake, we all HATE thunder and lightning. It's the worst thing in the world to us dogs. We were all inside, hiding under blankets and beds with the others," stated Fred Dog.

"The others?" Chake asked.

"Well, yeah, The Farmer, The Farmer's goldfish, and Old Dale," Fred responded.

"Dale? Dale the Dog is still alive?" Chake was stunned in asking.

"Of course, he is. He doesn't get around too much anymore, but he's still a great storyteller," Fred revealed.

"CC…"

"Yes, Chake?"

"It would've been impossible for any of these dogs to have set fire to the barn. No matter how we feel about them, scratch them off the list."

Chake wasn't about to be best friends with The Farmer's Dogs. Still, this investigation had to be based on fact, so he set aside his personal feelings as their alibis checked out. "The dogs are innocent, but there's one last thing I have to do before we leave here." Chake cryptically tells CC.

"What's that boss?" CC curiously wondered.

"Stay here, I'll be right back…" Chake hopped off the doghouse and strolled through the middle of where the dogs stood. With his snake tail slithering back and forth, he aimed his direction towards The Farmer's house. He had all sports of memories rushing back to him from his days of being a small chick living inside the house. He felt proud that he and CC were able to stand up to the dogs and teach them a lesson. So many times, inside of the house, inside that small coup, they would torture him. But there's one dog left that he felt he HAD to confront… Dale.

Back in the day, he used to escape the coup and the house and roam around the farm at night while everyone slept. He'd then pick the locks on the doors with his talons and hop back into his little coup without anyone knowing. This time, he didn't care who was watching; he had to see Dale.

"What are you doing? You can't go in there!" barked out Garrett the Dog.

"Yeah, I kind of agree, Chake? What are you doing, man?" agreed CC.

Chake said nothing in return. He flapped his wings wildly and etched his talon into the lock on the front door. A clicking sound let Chake know he was successful. He then latched onto the doorknob and swung downward, slowly creaking the door open. Without looking back, Chake went inside.

As always, after a long, hard day's work, The Farmer was passed out on the couch with a half-finished beer in one hand and a newspaper spread out over his pot belly. He was still wearing his farming clothes and dirty brown hat while his heavy, rumbling snores filled the room. Chicken Snake thought to himself, "Wow, this place hasn't changed at all." Even his old coup from years ago was still sitting there. He walked past the goldfish, who looked confused to see a new face. He searched around the house room by room, looking for Dale until he heard another loud snore coming from the opposite direction than The Farmer's.

Somehow, he knew, he just KNEW, it was him.

He entered a room lit up only by a crackling fireplace. He followed the snoring as it got louder, and sure enough, on the other side of the chair in the room… it was him…

"Wake up…" Chake said sternly.

Dale woke up at once with a loud snort. He shook the sleep away and cast his blurry eyes on the one standing before him. As his vision focused, he became more familiar with who had woken him.

"Chicken Snake?" he said in an old raspy voice. "It can't be."

"Yeah, it's me, Dale. You're looking… well… old." Chake set the tone.

"It happens to the best of us." Dale chuckled while trying to stand but gave up and lay back down.

"I would've guessed The Farmer would've sold you to a traveling circus sideshow a while ago," said Dale amidst a wide yawn.

"Nope, I'm still here, Dale. My buddy and I just laid down a nice Cluck and Slither on your boys out front. I couldn't believe they just happened to mention that my mom's mortal enemy was still kicking inside. Just unbelievable," Chake said while walking around the room, admiring how messy The Farmer truly was.

"So, are you here to finish what your mother started?" Dale asked.

Chake laughed. "No, Dale, not today, at least," he joked. "I've heard stories from others who knew my mom in the chicken coup and around the barn. I even remember some of the things you would say about her. But that's all that I have. Of course, as you know, my mother and my father died when my egg was laid; I was hatched without knowing anything about either of them. I thought that maybe…" Chake paused to collect his thoughts.

"You want me to tell you about your mother?" Dale softly asked.

"You're the only one left, Dale. I know you and my mother were each other's worst enemies, but sometimes you know your enemies better than you know your closest of friends," Chake said, finally meeting eyes with Dale.

"You've grown into a wise Chicken Snake. Dare I say I'm almost proud. And you look a lot like your mother… well… except for the scaly green tail, of course," Dale said, laughing. "Sit down by the fireplace, Chicken Snake. I'm too old and too tired to be roaming the yard and herding the sheep anymore, but I still have my wits about me. The one thing I can still be accused of is telling a pretty decent story; the story I tell about your mom is one of my absolute favorites."

Chake sat by the warm fire that lit up half of Dale's face. He was excited to be the one hearing a story instead of telling the story for once. Dale cleared his throat, stretched his front paws, and settled into story mode.

"Let me start off by saying, respectfully, your mother was a major pain in my butt." For some reason, this made Chake smile proudly. "While all of the other chickens stayed where they were supposed to be, she would flop around The Farm constantly of her own free will. She hops the fences and gets into all kinds of trouble. It's always been the job of the dogs to keep order and police the animals, which is a hard enough job, but she made out job ten times as difficult."

Dale continued. "The thing that no one really understands is that if we don't do our job and make the population here fear us dogs and respect us, then the entire system would fall apart. This is why we train to be vicious and mean. We don't really have anything against anyone on the farm, but we have to put on a show and appear as though we'll tear anyone apart who steps out of line.

"Now, those guys outside today take it a little too far at times. I do my best to keep them grounded and make sure they remember they're here to do a job, but I can only do so much these days." It all made sense to Chake, and all of a sudden, he almost felt bad for what he and CC did to them outside.

He ALMOST felt bad.

Dale continued. "Your mom may have been an extra load of work for us dogs, but we all respected her greatly. She would pick locks, visit her friends all over The Farm, slice open grain bags for the chickens, and even play pranks and set traps. One time, she placed a long shovel in front of the door. As soon as The Farmer walked out, he tripped over it and fell face-first into a cherry pie he was holding. I have to say I haven't laughed so hard in my entire life.

"When the farmer stood up, the entire pie was stuck to his face. He was so mad. We all had to hide out in the dog houses until he was done laughing. And then, of course, there was the whole incident with the cattle prod and her dressed up like a ghost."

"I'm actually well aware of that one, Dale." They both shared a laugh.

"Well, here's something you might not have known. Even though your mother and I clearly didn't like each other, I was there on that fateful day at the fence line. I frantically tried to separate her from that vile snake. And to be perfectly honest with you, the snake didn't choke to death like the legends I've heard that say that. He could've easily, with time, swallowed her; he died after I bit him."

Chake was stunned. He had completely made up the part about Simon the Snake choking to death. He also made up the name Simon for the snake.

"I don't know what to say, Dale. You tried to save my mom?"

"I tried, but I failed. As much as she drove me insane while she was alive, I was heartbroken to watch her go. I only wanted to keep her safe, to keep everyone safe. That was my job. She just had to go hopping the main fence that day.

"I've never forgiven myself for not doing my duties to the best of my abilities on that day. Also, I was there when the crows came and stole the other egg. Another crow had your egg in its clutches, but he dropped it when I chased him away. It was me that brought you to The Farmer. So, I'm glad you've sought me out. It gives me a chance to say I'm sorry. I truly am sorry, Chicken Snake."

Dale looked away from Chake and into the fire. Chake stood up and walked over to Dale. He put his wings over Dale's calloused paw.

"I'm sorry, too, Dale. I was so wrapped up in my own version of this story that I never imagined that your side would also make sense."

Dale and Chake spent another hour talking and laughing over old stories of Chake's mother. He went into the house expecting a confrontation, and he left with a new friend and a new respect for the dogs. He also felt as though he finally knew who his mother was… she was just like him.

Chake crept out of the house and back into the front yard, where he saw something he'd never imagined seeing in a million years. CC was throwing a stick across the yard, and all of those vicious evil dogs that they nearly had to fight to the death were wagging their tails faster than he could see, their sloppy tongues hanging out of giant smiles and chasing the stick until it landed, then bringing it back to CC.

"What's going on out here?"

Chake was confused.

"They call it 'Fetch'! It's a lot of fun. You should try this!" CC replied.

"How'd it go in there?" he asked.

"It really couldn't have gone any better, CC. I'll tell you all about it on the way back to the cow field."

CC tossed the stick one last time; this time, Garrett Dog caught it midair. They entered the yard ready for combat, and they left the yard with promises to come back and play more fetch. On the way home, Chake told CC everything about Dale, his mom, and the story of The Farmer's Dogs. CC was stunned by all of this new information.

"Funny thing," said CC. "The real story is even better than the one you made up."

Chake agreed. It was late; the moon was a sliver, and both Chake and CC were beyond exhausted. They briefly chatted about tomorrow's investigative activities.

"Sheep in the morning?" asked CC."

"Yep, Sheep," confirmed Chake. They bid each other a goodnight and went their separate ways.

CHAPTER 8
Good Morning Sheep

Breakfast time was always a happy time on The Farm. The Farmer never got enough credit from the community for his hard work. Right on time every sunrise, he would make sure everyone had enough to eat. While some took it for granted, CC was always happy to see The Farmer. He always thought that they had some sort of connection even though he and The Farmer couldn't understand one another. He seems to pay a little more attention to him than the other cows. This is why he always felt special.

The Farmer made him feel like he wasn't just another ordinary cow, which led him to believe he was half Chupacabra, which THEN led to meeting Chicken Snake and then to everything that has happened since.

So, CC respected The Farmer for his hard work and dedication to The Farm, and now he even credits him in a small way for making him the cow he is today.

Cow was also grateful to be awake. While the confrontations with the dogs were mentally draining at first, as well as the entire first day of the investigation, his dreams were again frightening.

The legend of The Cow Tippers was very real to the bovine population on The Farm. Sure, it could've all been made up. Since he's met Chake, he's realized that the lines between truth and fiction are indeed blurry. Just days ago, he thought he was an ordinary cow and that The Farm was the center of the world. He believed in every word of The Chicken Snake Story, that the dogs were cruel and evil and that The Old Red Barn would stand forever. This morning, he woke up knowing that nothing is certain and anything is possible.

Be that as it may, The Cow Tippers often invaded his dreams in the same exact way. He'd hear them laugh, watch them hop over the fence, slowly grow closer and closer as he froze in fear, unable to move and yell for help. And always right as they were inches away from his side with hands pressed outward, he'd wake up chilled and quivering.

Last night was no exception. It seemed as though they got closer with every dream. But CC had no time to think too much about any of that.

Today was Day Two of being a detective on the case of The Barn Fire. So, he hoofed his way across the fields, grabbed some delicious wheat for a quick breakfast, and made his way over to the fence shared by the henhouse field.

Chake adjusted a new tie that he woke up early and made out of fabrics he found inside The Farmer's house last night as he left.

"Good morning, CC!" he yelled as CC reached the fence.

CC yawned, "Morning, Chake."

"Man, you look like you didn't sleep a wink last night," noticed Chake.

"Well, it was hard to calm down from everything that went down yesterday, and then these nightmares..." CC muttered.

"Nightmares?" Chake asked.

"Oh, never mind that. I'm here, I've got the notebook, and I'm ready," CC mustered up.

"Well, good. We've got a lot on our plate today. And just remember, dreams are just your mind's way of telling its own stories when you're asleep. Just because your body needs rest doesn't mean your mind does. I've learned that all you need to do is take control of your dreams and have a little fun with them. If something in your dream scares you, if nightmares take over, turn it around, and you be the scary one. You'll feel much better and might even get some better sleep," Chake instructed.

"You're one clever chicken, Chake. I'll give it a shot next time."

Chake flapped his way onto CC's back. "Sheep time," he directed. "Hope you don't mind if I hitch a ride."

"Hold tight, Chake. It's gonna be a long, bumpy ride."

The sheep were moved to a somewhat distant enclosure. Before, they were usually lumped in with the cows, but since the barn burned down, there simply wasn't enough room for everyone. There was still a huge pile of black smoking debris that The Farmer continued to hose water over as he slowly removed shovel full by shovel full. But that whole area needed to be fenced off for safety, so the sheep were given their own spot along with the only goat on The Farm.

With The Farmer so busy tending to barn issues and the regular duties around The Farm, it was easier than expected to travel unnoticed throughout the entire Farm. The dogs noticed, but due to newfound respect and, dare we think, friendship, they knew what CC and Chake were doing and let it slide.

Sheep have a distinct language that sets them apart from anyone else on The Farm. They spoke in a high-pitched voice that annoyed CC when they all began talking at once, much like they were doing as they drew nearer the new sheep field.

The sheep are extremely simple residents of The Farm. As always, they were harmlessly passing their time in the grassland away until one noticed them heading down the hill in their direction.

"Hey! It's Chicken Snake and that cow that's also another thing that we can't remember how to pronounce!" yelled a sheep once they were in view.

"Chupacabra, he's half cow, half Chupacabra! Remember that!" Chake hollered back.

"Are you here to BOTH tell us your stories? Hey everyone, gather around! It's story time!" he excitedly announced to the other sheep.

Random chants of "Hooray!", "This is going to be great!", "Impressive!", and "Save some room for me!" all cluttered loudly.

Chake hopped up to a hay bale.

"Actually, sheep…"

"And goat!" the only goat on The Farm reminded him.

"And goat," Chake corrected himself. "Today, I want you all to tell US a story."

"But we don't have any stories. We're just simple sheep," barked a sheep named Tree. You see, Sheep weren't known to be the smartest animals on The Farm. As a matter of fact, some might say that in the intelligence department, they were ranking rather low.

Sheep only had names once they were old enough to speak. And whatever their first word was, that became their name. For example, this sheep's name was "Tree" because his first word was spoken as he ran into a tree while running around the field. Other sheep had names such as "Mom", "Barn", Eat", Ouch", and even "Farmer". The rest of The Farm community never passed judgment or spoke poorly about the sheep, but it makes sense to explain this before the sheep investigation goes any further; otherwise, it might get a little confusing.

"We're not asking you to tell us about an amazing adventure. We're asking for the truth," Chake pointed out with better detail as to what they hoped to hear.

"We all lost our homes in the barn. It's affected all of us, from The Farmer down to the field mice. We are on a quest to find answers. We want to know who did this and why."

"But why would we burn down our own home?" asked a sheep named Truck.

"That's what we'd like to know. Over the years, it's become very clear that none of you sheep…"

"Or goat!" the only goat on the farm chimed in once more.

"Okay, it's been clear that none of you very much liked The Farmer. We need to know if that dislike would be strong enough to do something so drastic and devastating as burning down the barn," Chake said as he stared over the crowd of sheep and one goat.

"Well, you're right about not liking The Farmer too much. None of us care too much for him."

"Wait!" yelled CC. "I remember overhearing all of you saying you had a plan to get even with The Farmer. It was a big rumor for a long time when you were sharing the fields with the cows."

"Yeah, yeah, we HAD a plan, but it had nothing to do with the barn," said Rock the Sheep. "The reason none of us like The Farmer is pretty simple. We sheep consider ourselves stylish animals. We love to grow our wool out as big and as puffy as we can get it. It's a real status symbol. The bigger and bigger it grows, the more popular that particular sheep is.

"But of course, right when we're starting to look incredible, that darn Farmer comes by with those shears, and we're back to the bald look that is utterly unflattering on a sheep.

"I mean, look how amazing we all look right now! Since The Farmer has been busy with the barn fire, he hasn't had time to rob us of our wonderful fluffy wool. But we know it's coming. I don't know what he does with all of that fabulous wool, but he can't seem to get enough of it."

"THAT is why you hate The Farmer?" asked Chake.

"Yep, imagine how you'd feel if he came by and plucked your feather every other week. And let me tell you, those shears are painful!"

CC then asked, "Well, what was your secret plan to gain revenge on him?"

"Funny enough, we never actually made the plan. It was just an idea that we'd always talk about. It certainly had nothing to do with burning anything down," said Water the Sheep.

"Well, what was the plan? Chake pressed.

Another sheep named Poop stepped forward. "Poop... Yeah, I know..." Poop the sheep explained. "We had always talked about ganging up on The Farmer during one of the Shearing sessions, holding him down and shaving his head just like he's shaved us so many times. But none of us knew how to work the shears or even take his hat off. So, while it's still fun to talk about, it'll probably never happen."

"Did you also happen to notice that The Farmer is mostly bald?" added Chake.

"Well, dang it! I've never seen him without his hat."

The sheep grumbled amongst themselves for a moment, realizing that their revenge strategy had some major flaws.

Chake broke up the chatter.

"Well, can you sheep..."

"And goat!" repeated once more, the only goat on the farm.

"Can ALL of you at least tell us where you were on the night of the fire?"

"They were in the barn right next to me," said CC. "I don't remember everything that happened that night, but once the fire woke me up, I recall seeing the entire flock."

"That's right, we were inside the barn! Lucky for us, that fire didn't catch our wool. We sheep are quite flammable!"

"Okay, CC, take the sheep..."

"And..."

"Yes, AND the goat off the list."

CC obliged and closed his notebook on the sheep as possible suspects.

"So, if you could imagine anyone on the farm doing such a terrible thing like burning down the barn. Who would it be?" questioned Chake.

"Probably the dogs! They've been nipping at our heels and chasing us around for years!" said a sheep named Bird sternly.

"The dogs have already been cleared, and I don't think you're going to have to worry about the dogs anymore, but just cooperate with them. They're just doing their job."

The sheep and the only goat on the farm looked a tad confused, but then again, they always looked confused.

"What about The Crows?" said Sheep the Sheep. "They just left before you got here."

"Yeah, one of them said he knows a secret about you, Chicken Snake."

"About me?" He was taken aback.

"Yeah, they said you and the Chup...Chuppacow...Chu, um, that cow would be here asking questions."

CC and Chake looked at each other as if they were the lead they were waiting for.

"CC, add the Crows to the top of the list. Looks like we're heading to the cornfields."

"Got any time to tell us that story from last night again?" yelled Achoo the Sheep, whose first word was a sneeze.

"Not today, everyone, and the next story we hope to tell is the story of how we broke this case wide open and brought justice to this farm."

Chake hopped back over the fence, back onto CC's back.

"I've heard terrible stories about the cornfields, Chake. Others have gone out there and never returned," CC nervously recalled.

"Well, whatever's out there hasn't seen a Chicken Snake and Chupacabra Cow enter the cornfields. And if the crows have a problem with us, we're about to settle that problem."

The cornfields were host to all sorts of legends and rumors. CC remembered a story about the dreaded Pumpkin Man that would roam the fields or the tale of a creature named Stump Drag who would rise from the nearby swamp at night and drag his victims back into his muddy, swampy home. They were both on high alert, knowing this would be an interesting part of the investigation.

CHAPTER 9
The Crows and the Cornfield

Even though it was still early in the day, the edge of the cornfields seemed dark and ominous. Even from a distance, the cornfield appeared to drain the light from the sky. It had the ability to change your good mood into a feeling of being unbalanced. Maybe it was just the unknown that chilled the spines of everyone on The Farm; perhaps that's where all the creepy stories came from. Either way, CC and Chake were at the edge of uncertainty as they stopped mere inches before entering.

Just within the cornfield, they could hear the scampering of small creatures and the flapping wings of birds that seemed larger than any they'd come across. The wind would whistle an eerie tune through the endless stalks of corn.

"How could any human need so much of this corn stuff?" CC thought to himself.

"Let's go inside," Chake said cautiously. The cornfield had no trails, at least none they could easily find.

It was a thick maze of maize. Every step they took resulted in a loud crunch beneath their feet and a cob of corn bouncing off their faces. They had no idea where the crows were, but they knew somewhere within this treacherous field is where they lived.

"Great place for such vile birds," Chake mumbled. Chake had long resented the crows now that Dale the Dog had confirmed that the crows flew away with the other egg, and even tried to take his as well. This was very personal.

And to think on top of everything, they have had something to do with the barn burning to the ground; it quickened his pace and helped him cast all fears aside.

CC didn't care too much for the crows, either. It wasn't personal, but he always looked at them as pests. They would always fly around The Farm, causing damage to The Farmer's crops. They never had a nice word to say about anyone. They constantly gathered in trees and "Cawed" at everyone for hours. It was just annoying.

While Chake was moving steadily with determination, CC, on the other hand, was growing more paranoid with every unexplainable movement or sound. He was letting this thoughts distract him from the task at hand.

"I'm not sure how much further I can go on Chake. Maybe we head back to the farm and wait for them to come to us," CC suggested.

"We've come this far, CC. If you'd like to turn back now, I'll understand, but this is something I HAVE to do," fired back Chake.

CC found comfort in Chake's forward drive and did his best to keep pace. After an hour or so into the cornfield, they'd yet to see another living creature. It's just the same vision repeatedly: corn.

Just then, a roar rang around the field. It was the familiar screeching call of the crows. There must've been hundreds of them, seemingly sounding an alarm of sorts. They both wondered if that alarm was to alert the other crows of their presence. With a few more crunching steps forward, a laughing voice whispered from the void.

"We see you…"

This startled even Chake.

"You've got a long nerve sticking your beak into the nest of The Crows."

"Show yourself!" screamed Chake.

"Don't mind if we do," laughed the voice. Suddenly, the corn stalks fell away in every direction, and a clearing opened around them as hundreds of crows dropped the camouflage they were holding. It was a trap, and they were completely surrounded.

"Well, if it isn't the Farm Star himself, Chicken Snake." The crowd roared with laughter. "Are you here to tell us your ridiculous story?" T

The leader of the Crows perched himself on an old, broken wooden fence hanging with rusted barbed wire. He introduced himself.

"I am Crowtan, ruler of these fields and General to my Crow Army."

All the crows had names that started with the word "Crow". It has been a custom with the crows for as long as there have been crows.

"For what do we owe the pleasure of your arrival?"

"There's no pleasure in us being here," Chake states. "We're here to get answers."

"Would this happen to be about your beloved barn blazing to ash? Such a pity." Again, the enormous crowd of crows chuckled.

"Tell us right now. Were you responsible for destroying our home!?" Chake asked, demanding an immediate reply. "Tell us NOW!"

"Oh, such a fiery attitude, Chicken Snake; you best be careful. You might burn down our home as well!"

CC butted in.

"Look, crows, it's obvious that we don't like each other, and we don't want to spend another second in this creepy cornfield. All we know is that you've been spying on our investigation, you've never had a nice thing to say about anyone on The Farm, and we've been told you're keeping a secret from Chicken Snake. Tell us what you know!"

"Or what Cow? Will you kick us around like you did those stupid dogs last night? Yeah, we see everything." Crowtan revealed. "Do you realize that at any given moment, I could mobilize their hungry warriors to attack the farm and tear everything and everyone apart?"

CC and Chake both glared with concern in their eyes. "The only reason I haven't made that order is because we gain necessary resources from The Farm.

"And not to mention, you animals AMUSE us. Life can be quite boring in the cornfields, but just a quick flight away is all the entertainment anyone could ever ask for."

The crowd erupted in laughter once more.

"Did you or did you NOT burn down the barn!?" Chake got back to the matter at hand at once.

"Oh, Chicken Snake, so determined, you very much remind me of your mother. Always venturing outside of her safety zone. Well, that didn't end up so well for her, did it? And you best mind your tone, you half-reptilian freak of your journey here will end up much the same!"

Chake and CC both bowed up, ready for what may be the last fight of their lives.

"Settle down, just… settle down…" Crowtan calmly suggested. "We're all much too exhausted for such a battle today. We're just coming off our annual Festival of Crows. It was a glorious carnival just a couple of farms west of here. We flew for miles to get there. We partied like mad children all that day and night, then flew miles once more to return to our cornfields.

"We saw the glow from a distance. As we got closer, we saw massive flames. We're just as curious to know how it happened as you are. But if you're asking if we took part in the devastation, I hate to admit that we did not."

Chake was not pleased with the realization that the crows were innocent. He thought for sure that this was where the case would end. But instead of solving it, he had CC scratch another name off the list. The possible suspects were dwindling, and he knew they were no closer to solving the case.

"The sheep said you had a big secret. What big secret?" CC asked. The cows all began to laugh yet again. Crowtan flew from the brown fence down to where Chake was standing.

"We go back a long, long way, don't we, Chicken Snake?"

"Yeah, we sure do. You and your crows stole the other egg my mother laid beside me; you even tried to steal mine as well. If you had your way, I would've never been hatched. I would've ended up being crow food like my brother or sister in the other egg."

The crows collectively giggled as if they knew something Chake did not.

"Is that truly where you believe that story ends? Oh, now that IS funny!" Crowtan laughed with his Army of followers. "Just when I think you farm animals cannot entertain me any further..."

"What are you talking about? What's so funny?" Chake fired back. "Yes, Chicken Snake, we grabbed the other egg and tried to grab you as well. But that mangy mutt Dale saved you from an entirely different fate. And yes, I must admit, those eggs were supposed to be part of a massive feast we had planned that afternoon. But a funny thing happened before dinner time. The other egg hatched."

"It hatched?!"

"Shockingly yes, it hatched right there on the Buffett, moments before my winged warriors were about to devour everything on it. But what came out of the shell was nothing we've ever seen."

Chake caught his breath, "What came out of the shell? Where is it now? TELL ME!"

His questions came out in rapid-fire form. Crowtan laughed and flew back to his perch on the fence.

"We don't take too well to orders or demands within our nesting grounds. If you care to know the answers you are looking for, maybe paying a nice visit to the snake pit on the other side of the dusty road might quench your appetites."

The crows laughed again, knowing that no one had ever returned from the snake pit.

"Haha, and you thought the cornfield was a scary place."

All of a sudden, CC and Chake were in the middle of a wind storm brought on by the flapping wings of a thousand crows. They shot straight into the sky without another word or clue about the bombshell they had just dropped on Chake. In a matter of moments, they were utterly alone in the cornfields once more.

"The snake pits?" CC asked. "I once had a friend who was a brave hawk. He mentioned seeing a large, deep, dark hole in the ground just across the dirt road. He said it looked like hundreds of worms, enough to feed his family for months. He said he was going to take a closer look the next day. The next morning, I watched him fly off. I watched him dive until he seemed to disappear into the ground. He never came back up. I never saw him again. He entered the pit where the snake that bit my mother was from. I just know it. It's the snake pit."

"You can't seriously be thinking about going there, are you?" CC wondered. "We already have one case to solve. That'll be another one for another day. But if I have a brother or a sister out there, the snakes know where they're at. I have to," Chake said in stunned thought. "But for now, let's get out of this cornfield and back on track."

A fluttering from above started getting closer and closer until another crow appeared out of nowhere. Chake and CC braced for a fight, but the crow quickly dismissed any danger they might have felt they were in.

"Hey guys, No, it's cool, it's cool."

CC and Chake relaxed their stance.

"Look, guys, my name is Crow Jack, and I didn't want to say this in front of the other crows, but I'm a big fan of you, Chicken Snake. I'm never too far away when you're telling your story, and I've always wanted to meet you face to face."

"Well, I appreciate that Crow Jack, but please excuse me. We have a lot of work to do," obliged Chake.

"Well, that's why I had to fly over here before you left the fields. I might have some information from you about your case."

"Okay, we're listening." Chake perked up.

"The place we hold the Festival of Crows also recently had a barn fire. It wasn't as bad as your barn fire, but it still caused a lot of damage.

When all was said and done, they found out quickly who was at fault." Crow Jack explained.

"Well, who was it?" Both CC and Chake asked simultaneously.

"Within every barn, there's a WAR going on inside the walls. The mice and the termites. They fight over territory, food, and sometimes just to fight. Apparently, one of those warring factions chewed through electrical wires in an attempt to make a weapon against the others, and it somehow started a fire."

"What's electrical mean?" CC asked, never having heard that term before.

Chake answered for the crow. "It makes the lights go on without lanterns, the tools, the TV, and basically everything inside The Farmer's house. I'll explain later."

Crow Jack continued. "So maybe, just MAYBE, it had something to do with that." Chake appreciated the tip. He even signed an autograph for Crow Jack on a fallen cornstalk leaf.

Before the crow flew away, he mentioned, "Be careful if you go to the Snake Pit. We've lost more than one crow who even got close to that place."

"IS whoever came out of the other egg there?" Chake asked as he flew higher.

"Only Crowtan knows for sure, but if his stories are true, then yes…"

Crow Jack disappeared in the blue sky that was shrouded by overhanging smothering corn.

Chake was perplexed. He was torn between finding the mice and termites, which might possibly solve this crime, OR taking the same path his mother took across the dirt road and entering the Snake Pit.

"I know what you're thinking right now, Chake," CC said, interrupting the silence. "And I completely understand why you're thinking what you're thinking."

Chake looked up a CC. "And I'll have you know, when it's time to go to The Snake Pit, I'll be right by your side. But first things first, buddy, we've got to finish this case. We've only got a few left to question. Which means we're getting closer to finding out who did it."

"Or closer to realizing we might never know," Chake interjected.

"Stay positive, Chake. Think about it this way: we faced the dogs and survived this cornfield. Nothing can stop us from solving this case.

Eventually, we'll learn what secrets are hidden in that snake pit. You and I, together, Chake."

Chake appreciated everything CC said, and it boosted his confidence. They took their final crispy, crunchy step out of the cornfield and headed back to The Farm. They had some bugs and rodents to question.

CHAPTER 10

The War Within the Wall

As many years as everyone had spent inside the barn, no one knew exactly what was happening inside the walls. Sure, the field mice would come and go, and spiders and other insects would crawl around and live their own lives without much interaction with the general population. Sometimes, CC would kick over a log and reveal a colony of termites feasting and nesting. But no one really knew if they had names or duties; they certainly had no idea an epic war was going on.

"I have no idea where we're going to find either the termites or the mice," Chake realized as they drew nearer to the cows' grazing field. "They all live within the walls of the barn now that the barn is gone, I really don't know where they've gone."

"I guess we'll just have to ask around," said CC as he looked around the horizon.

They retraced the steps of their investigation thus far. Neither the cows nor chickens had seen either of them. The Farmer's Dogs sniffed their way throughout their yard, even searching inside and around the perimeter of The Farmer's house. Nothing. It took a while to explain what a termite or field mouse was to the sheep, but once they remembered, their area also came up empty. They didn't tread back to the cornfield, knowing that both bugs and mice were an easy snack for the crows. They'd be foolish to choose that area to camp out.

CC went over to the firewood, which was still damp from the storm. He kicked over a few logs and saw nothing. It didn't make sense. There were thousands of termites and hundreds of field mice.

"They couldn't have just disappeared," Chake thought.

"Maybe they WERE responsible for the fire and just fled the scene once the damage was done," CC conspired.

Just then, the hay wagon collapsed, sending one of his giant wooden wheels rolling by right past them. CC and Chake together walked up to the fallen wagon they considered center stage for storytelling time.

CC kicked over the now one-wheeled wagon and revealed the termites... only there weren't that many.

CC recalled the termite population being so massive it would be impossible to count, but under the wagon resided seemingly less than a hundred or so.

"Hey, put that wagon back!" a small voice creaked.

"The sun is too bright! Cover us back up!" pleaded another.

"Not until you answer a few questions," Chake demanded as his shadow eclipsed the termites.

"Questions? What questions do you have for us termites? Can't you see that things are hard enough for us?" a termite named Tiktik desperately responded.

"Where are all of the rest of you?" CC didn't want to ask but still went ahead.

"They're dead, okay? The barn fire wiped most of our colony out," Tiktik sadly announced. "We were the only ones lucky enough to bury ourselves underground during the fire. We have nothing left, and now you want to ask us questions?"

"I'm very sorry to hear about your loss. I don't know what to say," CC solemnly offered his condolences. "Look, I can't imagine the suffering you've already endured, but I have to ask some questions so we can find out why this happened and maybe find out who did it," Chake said respectfully. "We understand that the termites and mice have been in an eternal battle inside the walls. Wars between you on distant farms have almost burned down other barns. I have to ask you if this war is what burned down our barn..."

"That war is over, Chicken Snake..." said a squeaky voice behind Chake. It was a small group of mice still charred from the fire, their fur stained in ash and struggle.

A field mouse named Shrill stepped forward. "Much like the termites, we lost nearly everyone sleeping in the walls of the barn. So, there's nothing left to fight for. We've been roaming the grounds of The Farm, looking for food and shelter. We heard you were looking for us."

"We were looking for both you and the termites to ask you questions about the night of the fire. We're asking everyone on The Farm what they knew or if they saw anything," Chake said and nodded to CC, "But we'll mark you both off the list. You've both lost more than anyone else." CC scratched the termites and the mice off the list and put the pencil behind his ear.

"Don't get us wrong, we have every reason to get even with The Farmer," said Tiktik the Termite. "The poisons, the sprays, throwing away the rotting wood that we related to the nest. But we'd never do something that would devastate our own or the rest of the animals."

"Not to mention the mouse traps all over the barn, all around The Farmer's house. I mean, what did we do that was so wrong?" Shrill hammered to the point. "And even though the mice and termites have always been in a fight for resources and territory, on this farm, it's never been violent. It was a big barn, and we managed with what we had. Now, we're all in this together." Shrill the mouse stepped into the termite lair and shook leg to leg,

"Truce?" Shrill asked hopefully.

"Truce," Tiktik affirmed. And just like that, the heated rivalry between the termite and field mice was officially over, at least on their particular farm.

"There's plenty of room for you and your family here under this wagon if you need a temporary home," Tiktik offered. Shrill accepted the offer, and while on other farms, the two species may be locked in combat, here they're sharing whatever they had left.

"Hey, guys," a field mouse yelled up to CC and Chake. "I don't know if this means anything to you, but on the night of the fire, I was looking out of the window before I fell asleep. I've always enjoyed watching storms. I noticed that the pigs were already out there. They were laughing and rolling around. Like I said, it might be nothing, but then again, it might be something."

Chake thanked the mouse for the tip before CC pushed the wagon back over the smallest members of the farm community, pleased with the resolution of their storied conflict, but with no new answers, no new clues, and as the sky grew dark once more, nowhere near solving the case again.

An obviously frustrated Chake looked downward at the steps he was taking back to the chicken field. CC moped in much of the same manner.

"Pigs and Horses tomorrow?" asked CC,

"Pigs and Horses tomorrow," he replied in a monotone voice. Chake sat in his bedding area and stared at the star-filled sky. He was hungry but didn't eat, tired but didn't sleep. He wondered if he had a sibling out there. Was he or she right across the dirt road this entire time? He knew he HAD to go to the Snake Pit eventually, maybe even as soon as tomorrow.

CC was also exhausted. What an adventure he had today. From the sheep to the cornfield, the crows to the unification of the termites and field mice. He had a late dinner and then stammered over to his usual sleeping spot. He remembered what Chake said to start the day; he was ready for the dream tonight if it decided to materialize in his head.

"Just relax and take control of your dreams." He quietly motivated himself. "Just relax and take control...of... your..."

CC passed out. But before it felt like he slept even a minute, CC opened his eyes. He heard what sounded like the rattling of the chain link fence that operated The Farm and the dirt road.

There it was again!

"Am I dreaming again?" he asked himself as he felt his body tense up and freeze.

"Ching Ching."

The fence shook again.

"Okay, relax, cow, just relax," he whispered. He heard human voices creeping up behind him. Slowly, he heard their footsteps in the crisp grass.

"Okay, cow, take control, just take control." He repeated like a mantra. Suddenly, he felt as if he regained control of himself. Each leg was raised one by one, freeing themselves from the ground; he remembered how he felt facing down Garrett the Dog, how he felt being surrounded by the crows. Now, it was time to turn this nightmare into something a little fun.

But just then, he felt the force of six human hands press against his side, his balance left him, and the cold sting of the terrain crashed against his other side.

"This isn't a dream!"

He struggled to his feet and called out for help.

"The Cow Tippers are here! Help!"

As soon as he got back to his feet, they ran towards him again with hands outstretched, as he'd seen so many times in his dreams. Again, they pushed him with all their strength, and he landed hard on the ground to a chorus of their laughter.

By this time, the entire Farm was awake and watched in horror. Chake flapped over the fence and headed to CC as he struggled again to his feet.

"Stay Down!" he screamed as he recalled the story he told about CC's mother. Sure, he might have made up the entire thing, but he wasn't about to see that tragedy come to life.

CC made it back to his feet. The Cow Tippers again positioned themselves once more to deal with what could be one more fatal push. Suddenly, out of the darkness of night came The Farmer's Dogs, who easily hopped their fence and stood between CC and The Cow Tippers. At the same time, Chake arrived, as well as every other cow in the field. The three humans were completely surrounded.

Chake launched at the Cow Tippers first and wrapped nature's gift of a snake's lower half around the neck of a young blonde-haired human while pecking him in the nose as hard as he could. All five dogs grabbed ahold of the second chubbier human, ripping his clothing and dragging him around the field. The other cows found strength in numbers and stampeded the third human as he ran for his life back toward the fence. The rest of the farm was watching from beyond the fences until...

" BANG!"

The Farmer shot his long boom stick into the air while standing on his porch. Everyone's heart skipped a beat at the same time. With flashlight in hand, The Farmer made his way over to where the attack took place. He said something to the three roughed-up humans and pointed his boomstick in their direction. They didn't dare move.

Chake quickly flapped over the CC, who was in pretty bad shape.

"You okay, buddy?" he asked.

"I don't know, let me try to stand up."

He got halfway to his feet and fell back over. "Nope, not okay at all, Chake."

The dogs stood guard with The Farmer until several of the human wagons with crazy flashing lights showed up and took the three humans away. The Farmer looked over CC; the look on his face wasn't too assuring. CC looked up at Chake again; he spoke weakly and softly.

"Are you sure this wasn't all a dream?"

CC then closed his eyes.

"CC? CC?!?" Chake yelled at his friend, but the Farmer and the dogs began to shoo everyone back to their designated areas. Chake stayed with CC as long as he could, but even he was placed back into his own field. Outside of the constant waving of flashlights, darkness covered everything that happened to his friend that night.

"Please be okay," he said to himself again and again until his voice went dry. He thought he saw multiple flashlights beaming in various directions; maybe more humans had come to help. He watched for as long as he could stay awake, but sleep eventually won. With the crow of a rooster, Chake's eyes burst open. He awoke looking to the same sight he fell asleep with. But with the morning light, he saw that CC was no longer lying in the field.

"He's gone..."

His first thought was to ask the dogs what they knew about his friend's whereabouts. He flapped over their yard, and the dogs were gone. He checked around the yard, scanning the farmlands for any sight of them, but nothing.

But he had one more dog to ask.

Chake picked the lock to The Farmer's house, once again following the snores to the last room on the right.

"Dale!"

Dale again awoke with a snort.

"Huh? Chicken Snake? Back so soon?"

"Dale, you have to tell me where The Farmer took my friend, the cow!"

Dale licked his paw and rubbed his eyes. "Oh, I heard about an unfortunate incident in the cow field. Some terrible humans came and..."

"Look, Dale, I know what happened. I was there. But I don't know what happened to my friend!"

Dale cut off Chake.

"Well, all I know is that my boys were really upset this morning. This is strange because, usually, when they go for a ride in the big truck, they're overly excited. So, I imagine your friend was on that truck."

Chake's heart sank.

"Dale, have you taken that ride on the big truck?"

"Many times, it was my favorite part of being a pup. I'd hang my head out the window and just wag my tongue in the most wonderful breeze." Dale recalled. "We've always been told that the big truck takes us to The Great Farm, where we all spend the rest of our days relaxing and living the best life we could ever imagine."

"Is this true? Is there a Great Farm?"

"Well, usually when we get there, we have to stay in the truck, but I can tell you it's a HUGE place. Didn't look too much like a farm, but it's the size of 100 farms," said Dale to the best of his recollection.

Just then, Chake began to accept the hard fact that he'd probably never see CC again. He bid Dale a farewell, left The Farmer's house, hopped back into his coup, and just sat there for hours. He hoped at any minute, the big truck would pull up, and a happy, healthy CC would dance his way out of the back, but he stayed in the same place as that day wasted away. No truck. No CC.

It was clear that his friendship with the Chupacabra Cow meant more to him than anything else. He hadn't thought about the investigation; the Snake Pit never even crossed his mind. He would just sit and wait.

CHAPTER 11
Down, on the Farm

The afternoon lunch bell rang. Chake hadn't eaten all day, nor had he spoken a word to anyone on The Farm.

"You've got to snap out of it, Chake," said Vinnie the chicken. "CC may be gone, but you're still here. The rest of us are still here. They look up to you. If you're down in the dumps, it's going to bring everyone down with you."

"I know, it's just not fair. He's my best friend, so full of life, so innocent. It's just not fair," Chake said, speaking for the first time all day. Looking around, Chake realized that The Farm seemed to have a grey cloud over it. Everyone was upset, depressed, saddened, and not sure what to say or do. Though The Chupacabra Cow story was brand new, between that and the investigation, CC had at once captured the hearts of everyone on The Farm.

"Don't you have a case to solve?" Vinnie questioned.

"To be honest, Vinnie, I don't think I can do it without him. We made a great detective team. It was like all the crime shows I'd watch in The Farmer's House when I was just a little chick. But even with him, we still had no real leads or solid suspects." Chake made it known that everyone he questioned thus far turned out to be innocent.

"So, you're giving up?" Vinnie asked.

"I don't know, I'm just...I don't know," he replied as if conflicted over what to do next.

"What would you tell your cow friend if he were in YOUR situation?"

The elder chicken asked.

"I would tell him, um... I guess I would tell him to never give up," Chake said as he rose to his feet. "You're right, Vinnie. CC wouldn't want me to sit here and mope all day. He'd want me to get off my tail feathers and pick it up where we left off." Chake became more inspired, as if CC was right next to him, cheering him on.

"Thank you, Vinnie. You've always been there for me. I'll make you AND CC proud. I'm going to solve this case!"

Chake took flight in the direction of the pig's new pen by the pond. He wasn't a strong flyer; chickens could only flap their wings for so long, but with the motivational wind to his back, he flew further and faster than he had ever flown before. A crowd of chickens and cows cheered. This case was still open!

As Chake got near the pig pen, his demeanor was all business. The smell of the pig's muddy field was never pleasant, and he'd never talked to a pig without getting mud splashed on him, but funny enough, he didn't care. He had questions that needed to be answered, and no smell or a splash of mud would stop him from getting those answers.

"Pigs!" he screeched, his voice carrying over the pigpen and beyond. "I have questions concerning the case of the Old Red Barn fire, and I want them answered immediately!"

The pigs stood in order, shocked by his tone in asking. They knew he wasn't there to mess around. The first pig to respond to Chake was a visibly nervous Jacob the Pig.

"How can we help Chicken Snake? We'll cooperate in any way you need us to."

Chake fired directly into his questions, speaking swiftly and sternly. "On the night of the barn fire, it was noticed that every pig standing here was already outside before the fire started. Once the fire started, everyone inside barely escaped! Actually, let me rephrase that: thousands of termites and hundreds of field mice did NOT make it out. The REST of us barely got out. Why were you safely outside while the rest of us were in danger?"

"Oh, geez, Chicken Snake. You don't think that we..."

"Just answer the question!" Chake cut him off and demanded.

"There was a storm that night, Chicken Snake. While we're not a huge fan of thunder and lightning or the crazy winds, we certainly love a nice muddy field!" explained Jacob Pig.

"Yeah, it hasn't been that muddy in months! It was great!" yelled out a pig that went by the name of Zoey, who stepped on a puddle and splashed mud all over Chake's feathers in the process.

"Ugh..." Chake thought as he wiped himself off as much as he could. "In the past, you've had grievances with The Farmer. You've even tried to break your fences and run away. Why?"

Jacob Pig replied with one word.

"Bacon."

"Bacon?" Chake asked.

"C'mon Chicken Snake, you've read just as many of the tracks papers as we have. THICK CUT SMOKED BACON from locally raised pigs." Every pig in the pen gulped with widening eyes. "We stopped believing in that Great Farm story years ago. Between the papers and what the crows have told us, we know that our time is here and now, so we try to make the most of it. If there's a sloppy, muddy field, we dance in it. When the slop comes, we savor every bite; if there's a rainstorm, we cherish every drop. I'm really sorry about what happened to your friend, and we're all sad about the barn, but the pigs had nothing to do with it."

Chake looked at the pigs in a whole new light. His doubts about The Great Farm outweighed his hopes that it existed. He had flashing thoughts of CC and thought, "If he's not at The Great Farm, where is he?" He immediately put his game face back on.

"Did any of you see anything? Maybe someone hanging around the barn that didn't belong there?" he asked.

"Well, we saw The Farmer and a dog locking down the place, we saw another cow taking a dump out by the fence, but that's all that we could really see. The wind and rain were crazy, made it hard to see."

Another pig named Bonzer stepped up.

"We did hear the horses yelling rather loudly at one point. I couldn't understand what they were saying. Figured they were just freaking out about the weather."

"Got it." Chake had heard enough from the pigs and believed their story. He looked over his shoulder as if to tell CC to scratch them off the list but stopped himself. "Thanks, pigs, keep your heads up high!"

"Hey, next time you stop by, let's hear that cow story again. Cool?"

"Well, hopefully, he'll be back someday soon to tell that story himself."

Chake flapped back to where the barn used to stand, took a left down a short trail, and ventured to the horse stables.

The horses are the most powerful and majestic of all animals on the farm. They're also the most stubborn and arrogant as well. But if they were to open up to anyone, it would be Chake.

The horses were just as big fans of The Chicken Snake story, even the new Chupacabra Cow story, as anyone. The fancy horses had even previously requested private storytelling sessions with Chicken Snake solely for horses.

Chake has always had a good relationship with them; their leaders, Leanne and Jenny, were once circus horses. They would dance and trot and perform everywhere. Once they retired, they came to the farm to live out their lives. No horse was ever taken away on the big truck, so, in some respects, THIS was their Great Farm.

All in all, there were about 23 horses on The Farm. Chake knew most of them on a first-name basis; he enjoyed watching them race around the small track they have just outside the barn area. But this wasn't a pleasure trip. As much as he respected the horses, they were the last ones on his list to be questioned.

Chake knew that if the horses were cleared, then the entire investigation would come up empty. He couldn't imagine the horses would ever pull something like this. They've always been so respectful and honorable. Still, even though the horses had a small space with the old barn and these stables out behind them, they have always had an issue with where the barn stood, and Chake knew what it was.

"Horses gather around!" Chake ordered. Some were feeding, some kicking up dirt on the track, others just wandering around their grounds.

"Hey, it's Chicken Snake!" excitedly announced a horse named Tay Tay. "Will this be the requested private storytelling we've been waiting upon?" Leanne Horse pondered in a snooty tone.

"We would also like a retelling of the cow story as well if you fancy," Jenny Horse also asked. "And please keep the others away. This is strictly for horses!"

"Listen, this isn't story time, okay? I need you to give me your complete attention."

"Well, if you're not here to tell the stories, I'll be off to complete my laps." Leanne headed back to the track.

"Excuse me! I'm not asking for your attention. I'm demanding it!"

The horses all looked a little stunned and slightly annoyed at Chake.

"Listen here, my fine feathered friend, we don't take too kindly to such disrespect. Therefore, I'll have to ask you to remove yourself from our stables," Jenny Horse insisted, but Chake held his ground.

"Over the past few days, we've lost the barn, fought the dogs, braved the cornfields and the crows, questioned my closest friend, and even had to fight off humans. Above everything, my best friend was hurt, and now I have no idea where he's at. So don't talk to me about disrespect! Just answer the questions I have, and I'll be on my way!"

"I'm truly sorry about your cow friend. We all became quick fans after you spoke of his journey in the barn that night. I'll gather the rest of us."

Leanne Horse rounded up each and every horse on the stable grounds.

"On the night of the barn fire, we learned that some horses were still outside before the fire sparked. We have to know where everyone was that night. I distinctly remember most of you were inside the barn during the story. Who was outside?"

Chake laid it out there for the horses to figure out.

"Well, that would be YOUR fault, Chicken Snake," Marci Horse said from the back. "We all planned on braving the storms in these stables. We've weathered many a rainy night and beautiful lighting shows in the sky within the stables. Sure, the wind was stronger than usual, but when nature offers us such a production, we rarely fail to spectate." "So, what does that have to do with me?" Chake was confused. "It's simple: once we all heard that you were going to tell a NEW story, we forgot about the storm. We packed as many of us into that barn as possible, but a few of us had to miss it; it was a sold-out show!"

Jenny Horse went on. "So, Leanne and I felt as though we should lead by example, and we stayed outside while our fellow horses enjoyed the show."

"We have reports of your screaming and neighing loudly."

"Oh, Chake, haven't you ever truly appreciated lighting? Back when we were on the circus show, they would light up the sky every night with something the humans called fireworks. Beautiful colors and gigantic sprawling flashes of wonder. All the humans would yell out in awe, "Ooh!" and "Ahhh!" We were simply doing much of the same," she explained. Chake was pleased that the horses were straightforward and mentally marked them innocent and off the list.

But they were the last on that list.

He had nothing.

After everything he and CC went through, the case was as wide open and unsolved as it was from the moment the fire started. He thanked the horses for their time and mosied back to his sleeping spot.

Again, night fell over The Farm, and again, he had no answers; again, CC was nowhere to be found. He regretted not saying goodnight to CC the night before. Sure, he was tired and frustrated with the case. Still, he took for granted that he'd have another night to say goodnight or maybe even tell him what a great job he was doing or how he considered him his very best friend.

"Never go to bed angry," he mentally noted. "Goodnight, my friend, wherever you are."

While the case was still open, this day had come to a close.

CHAPTER 12
The Snake Pit

Today HAD to be the day. He needed to take his mind off CC; the investigation was going nowhere, and nothing on The Farm was lifting his spirits. In Chake's mind, he had nothing left to lose.

"The Snake Pit." He said to himself. "I have to know."

He thought about his friend, the hawk, whom he watched enter the pit and never return. He thought about the crows that have lost many to the snakes. He thought about his mother and his entire story that was originally caused by the snakes.

He also thought about how CC said he'd be right by his side when he decided to go. But none of that was going to change his mind. If he had family in that Snake Pit, he was going to find out.

Not to mention, he was half snake.

From his belly to the end of his tail, he was a green, scaly, slithering, cold-blooded snake. If he had any chance at all, it would be due to the fact that he's pretty much one of them...pretty much.

Once again, a look of determination was etched on Chake's face. He hopped out of the chicken coup, crossed the cow's field, walked right by where he last saw CC, and, without hesitation, flew over the main fence around The Farm, clearing its height without touching it.

The next thing he knew, he was standing on the dirt road, looking towards the unknown on the other side. The rocks scraped against his scaly belly as his motions kicked up a small cloud of dust. Behind him, he heard a few cows yell, "Chicken Snake! What are you doing? Come back!"

He ignored them without even looking back. Inch by inch, the half-chicken crossed the road.

All of a sudden, he heard a collective hissing sound and rustling in the weeds ahead. This stopped Chake in his tracks.

"Am I doing something really, really stupid here?" he thought to himself as he decided to move forward. These are the very same steps his mother took on the very same day he was hatched and the very same day she died. He was hoping that both she and CC were with him in spirit. Every thought he had told him to turn around and run back to The Farm as fast as he could, but his steps finally took him to where the dirt road met the thick weeds on the other side. The hissing and slithering noises grew louder; the Snake Pit had to be close.

Once in the tall, brown, dead weeds, Chake kept seeing movement from the corner of his eyes. As soon as he'd look in a particular direction, there would be nothing there, only to catch a glimpse of something else moving in another direction. High above, he saw a couple of crows circle over his head, laughing, of course; they were always laughing. It seemed like the hissing sound was coming from everywhere; weeds would move in all directions. He felt surrounded and claustrophobic as if it were too late to turn back. He realized he was turned around and disoriented to the point where he wasn't sure which was home, even if he wished to go home.

The look of determination was gone; he was genuinely afraid. His wings shook, and his scales stood on end, knowing that every step forward could be his last.

Then, all of a sudden, the hissing stopped.

The movement in the weeds calmed.

It was quiet.

He took one more step forward...

The ground beneath his feet and snake tail gave way, and he plunged into a dark cavern. It seemed as if he was falling in slow motion as he watched the passing dirt and roots, as well as the broken weeds that fell with him. His landing was sudden, hard, and with a solid thud.

He got to his feet and shook himself off. Chake then noticed he was alone in a large underground arena of sorts, surrounded by thousands of holes in the dirt. Some holes were small, while others were much bigger; he instinctively knew what these holes were for. He'd often dream of gliding through such holes under the Earth; it must've been his snake intuition. Suddenly, the arena grew loud with those now-familiar hissing sounds that seemed to echo from each hole.

Chake stayed directly in the center of the room as he watched as hundreds of long, slithering, slimy snakes appeared from the holes.

With fangs showing and piercing stares, they made a complete circle around Chake.

Now, being half snake is one thing, but telling the story of the snake and his mother was another, but none of that prepared him for how terrifying this would be.

Once the massive and constantly moving crowd of snakes had entered the room, one last snake, a MUCH larger snake, peeked its head out of the biggest hole in the wall.

"Soooo, what do we have here?"

The largest snake looked over Chake as the others tasted the air around him with darting forked tongues.

"At firssst I thought we had oursssselves a lossst little chicken who just happened to wander into our sssupper time," he continued. "But now I sssee that you're a little more complicated than that." The giant snake stayed inside the wall while his slivered yellow eyes focused on the back half of Chake.

"My name is Chake. I am half chicken and, as you can see, half snake." Chake went on. "I didn't wander off The Farm, and I didn't accidentally find The Snake Pit. I came looking for it."

"You're quite the fool, aren't you. Normally, by now, my family would've been slowly digesting you, but I'm far too curious to hear your story, Chake, is it?"

Chake thought even in his darkest moment, people still wanted to hear the story.

"Yes, it's Chake."

"Well, go on, Chake. How does one become half chicken and have snake? And why have you entered our Pit?"

The walls seemed to move around him as hundreds of eyes seemed to thirst for him; this made speaking a formidable task, but he managed to spill out a short version of his story.

"My mother was a chicken, a chicken that one of your snakes tried to eat. Bottom line, my mother laid two eggs inside the snake, and later, I was hatched with both chicken and snake features."

"And what of the other egg?" The snake interrupted with a growing amount of interest.

"I don't know what happened to the other egg. It was taken by the crows. They're the ones who told me that I would find those answers here in The Snake Pit. THAT is why I'm here," answered Chake as the snakes began to look amongst themselves.

"Oh, thossse crowsss, ssso arrogant and yet ssso tasssty. If it weren't for thossse curiousss crowsss we might actually have to go out and hunt for our mealsss." The room filled with the most sinister laughter Chake had ever heard. "Well, Chake, sssince its answersss you ssseek, answersss you shall receive."

Chake braced himself to learn the fate of the other eggs. Even if it were the last thing he would ever learn, he was ready to know the rest of a story he had heard and told his entire life.

"Ssseveral yearsss ago, the crowsss did indeed find an egg. They brought it back to the cornfieldsss to connssume, but it hatched.

Inssside was something the likesss of what they'd never ssseen. "Much like you, Chake, it wasss half chicken and have gloriousss sssnake. Even at birth, this creature wasss a true warrior, he wasss meant to be their feassst, but instead, it wasss the crowsss that became the meal. He wrapped himsssself around one crow and dug hisss fangsss into his wing. The crowsss were unable to fight thisss amazing creature, ssso they trapped him and dropped him here in The Pit where he grew and grew into a leader, a leader that strikes fear in the hearts of all creatures great and small."

"So, the egg was my... my brother?" Chake was trying to put the pieces together. "Where is he? Is he still here?" Chake asked.

"Oh yes," the large snake revealed as he stepped from the hole in the wall. "I'm right here."

As the snake slowly emerged from the hole, Chake saw that his entire lower half was the mud-covered body of a chicken. It was his brother.

"You're my brother?" Chake was stunned as he asked.

While Chake was a chicken with a snake tail, his brother had a long snake head with a chicken's body.

"I never knew there wasss another. I was raisssed here in the Pit with my brothersss and sssisssters. I wasss known as The Crow Ssslayer. I became Leader of The Pit with ruthlesss aggression. And now, to my sssurpissse I have a brother."

"Do you have a name?" Chake asked.

"Sick... They call me Sick," said his brother.

Chake asked, "Because you're half snake and half chicken, like my name, but the other way around?"

"No, no, no, my brother. They call me Sick because I'm Sssick and demented. It'll be nice having an unexpected family member here in The Pit with usss. I'll teach you the waysss of the sssnakesss, and sssince we share the sssame blood, before long, you'll be as ruthlesss as I."

"I can't stay here, Sick. I have a home and a family on The Farm. What if you came with me? I'll show you a whole new world out there where there's sun and good people. You'll have no reason to be sick and deleted or ruthless," Chake replied.

"That all sssounds very nice, Chake, but you're not underssssstanding me. Thisss wasssn't an invitation, my brother. Thisss isss your new home."

Chake knew the dangers of coming to The Snake Pit; he truly expected the worst, but he never expected he'd be forced to call it his new home. Chake knew that he had to find a way out as soon as possible. While it was great that he conducted his goal of coming to The Pit and seeing his brother, there was no way he was about to set up shop and spend the rest of his life there.

He looked back at Sick and said, "It's been really nice to meet you, my brother," and started flapping his wings with everything he had.

"Get him!" Sick ordered.

The snakes began to thrust upward towards Chake. Two snakes coiled their bodies around each of his legs and pulled him back to the floor of The Pit.

"Try that again, brother or not, you will be consssumed!"

Chake felt helpless. He tried again to reach the daylight above, but this time, his brother wrapped his upper snake body around Chake and squeezed.

The breath was leaving his lungs.

"It appears that only I was gifted the strength of the mighty snake," Sick said while glaring into his brother's eyes. "I think this family reunion is over."

Sick opened his mouth as wide as it would go and pulled Chake closer to his fang-filled mouth.

Just then, a giant white and black leg slammed into The Pit, stomping out a bunch of the snakes. The Pit began to cave in, and several snakes fled back into their holes. The leg pulled out, and the opening to The Pit opened widely. Hundreds of war-faced crows entered The Pit in attack mode.

This was war.

Snake and crow bodies were being flung all around The Pit. Hissing and Cawing rang throughout the cavern and holes. During the commotion, Chake managed to loosen Sick's grip, wrap his own snake body around Sick, and squeeze him.

The two brothers were in a life and death struggle in the middle of the snake pit while the crow and snake battle surrounded them. Just then, the giant leg returned from above and scooped them both out of the hole in the ground. Both Chake and Sick released their grips and fell to the ground. Chake looked up at the large figure that had grabbed him. He was standing in front of the sun, and Chake could only see his silhouette.

"CC?" He was astonished. "CC!" he screamed in delight.

"Hey, Chake!" said CC, who all bandaged up. Chake wrapped his wings around him and smiled as if it were the greatest moment of his life, which it indeed had been.

"I thought you were gone forever! What happened?" Chake excitedly asked.

"Well, before I tell you that, would you mind telling me who that is?"

CC wondered as he looked over at Sick.

"That's my brother, Sick," Chake introduced to CC. "He was the other egg, and now he's the king of the snakes and was trying to eat me a minute ago."

Just then, a massive wave of crows left The Snake Pit and flew back towards the cornfield.

"My beautiful Pit, my family!" Sick said as he peered down into the large hole filled with what once was his kingdom and what remained of the other snakes.

"Maybe someday, when you're done trying to be so ruthless, you can cross the road and experience a better life," Chake said to his brother.

Sick didn't say a word. He looked at Chake for a few moments and then flapped his wings as he dived back into the remnants of his Pit.

"Well, there's one mystery solved. How's the case of Barn Fire coming along?" CC wondered as they walked across the road together and back onto The Farm.

"Forget about all of that! How did you know I was in The Snake Pit? I was literally an inch away from being snake food when you and the crows showed up! And how did you get the crows to come along? And are you alright? Where'd you go? I'm so confused right now! Start talking, cow!"

85

Chake fired off these questions one after another, talking almost too fast for CC to understand. CC explained that the big truck brought him back to The Farm. As soon as he stepped off the truck, the other cows told him that Chake had made the journey across the road.

CC knew that could have only meant one thing.

So, with the help of the cows, the dogs, and basically everyone on the farm, he broke down the fence and headed over to save him.

"See, I told you if you decided to go to The Snake Pit, I'd be right by your side. A little late, but better late than never." CC also mentioned that he bumped into Crow Jack the Crow as well, and they were already on their way to battle the snakes. So, the timing was just right.

Chake looked at Cow as The Farmer was trying to fix the trampled fence and smiled.

"CC, you may be half cow and half Chupacabra, but you're 100% my best friend."

CC laughed, "That was the cheesiest thing I've ever heard, Chake, but thank you."

CC and Chake were back together on The Farm, and it seemed like a light turned back on for everyone.

CHAPTER 13
An Average Ordinary Day on an Average Ordinary Farm

A few weeks after The Barn Fire and the investigation that followed, life got back to normal. Sure, the case was still unsolved, but everyone on The Farm was proven innocent. The Farmer and other humans were well into constructing a newer, bigger farm with enough room for everyone. He also rebuilt the silo and made major renovations to the horse stables. The entire farm community was buzzing with excitement as this farm and the community that called it home were living within its greatest days.

CC and Chake stayed the best of friends. Even though they weren't able to solve their first case together, they continued to take cases and solve crimes and mysteries even though The Farm had been a peaceful and honest place.

One time, Jeannie the Chicken sounded the alarm in the hen house. She swore that a fox had broken into the fields and attacked the chicken coup, but after a quick investigation, it turned out she was only dreaming. Case Solved. Another time, four of the barnyard cats named Larry, Allie, Jake, and Jodi stole a piece of rope from the stables. It was an easy crime to solve as all they had to do was follow the trail of cat hair to where they were hiding. Simple situations with simple solutions. But in the back of their minds, they still wondered who set the barn on fire.

Between cases, CC and Chake made sure that story time was a weekly barnyard tradition. Not only did they each tell their own stories, but they told the story of the entire investigation. They shared their adventures in the cornfield with the crows and the battle of The Snake Pit. Not only were CC and Chake center stage but even Dale the Dog made his way from The Farmer's House and told stories from long ago. Vinnie the Chicken got involved as well. Leanne and Jenny, the former circus horses, told stories of their road adventures before calling the farm their home. The mice and termites both shared how they were able to end their turf war. And basically, everyone had the opportunity to share their lives with the rest of The Farm.

One night, Crow Jack the Crow even flew in to tell the tales of the crows, and even Crowtan and other crows attended. Once Crow Jack was finished with his saga, everyone gave him a standing ovation. This built a bond between The Crows and The Farm that was long overdue in everyone's opinion. The night, when the crows took flight, they launched from the frame of the new barn being built and accidentally nudged a lit lantern, which fell to the ground and instantly caught a small pile of hay on fire. Thankfully, it was noticed and dealt with quickly as the cows stamped it out. In that very instant, CC and Chake looked at each other as though everything had just fallen into place.

"CC, are you thinking what I'm thinking?"

"Chake, I believe I am!"

They put together that there was indeed one lit lantern in the barn that night that was blowing back and forth from the wind that forced its way into the barn.

"Chake, that lantern was hanging right above where the fire started that night," CC remembered.

"CC, " Chake excitedly patted his friend on the head. "The wind must've blown the lantern off the hook..."

CC picked up where Chake left off.

"And it crashed on the ground below."

They concluded by saying in sync, "And that is why the Old Red Barn burned down!" Just like that, the case was solved, FINALLY!

As word spread throughout the farmlands, the animals made sure The Farmer remembered to blow out another lantern. Sometimes, they'd just blow it out themselves. A huge weight was lifted from the backs of both CC and Chake. They felt as though there was no case they couldn't crack. They finally had an ending to their ultimate story.

A few months later, it was storytime night again, but this time, it was inside their new giant red barn.

This place was amazing. The termites and mice peacefully moved into the walls; the crows even found a space in the attic and watched over The Farm from the skies. The horses had more room inside and out, and the pigs and sheep moved back home, as did the only goat on the farm.

Chake and CC went on together and told the stories of their childhoods; this time, they told them without having more factual information to share. They told the story of the Case of The Old Red Barn Fire.

This time, they had an ending.

As the night drew to a close, the crowd was ready to call it a night. Another voice cut through the barn.

"If you don't mind, I alssso have a ssstory to tell."

Chake's heart sang. "It's my brother."

No one knew what to think. They've never seen anything like this creature before. His long snake head and chicken body slithered through the crowd, who backed away, forming a path that cut its way through to the stage.

"Chake... My brother... May I?"

Chake was speechless, but he motioned to Sick that he was welcome to take the stage. Sick took the opportunity and made his way to the bales of hay they called a stage.

"I've lived my life in darknesss, sssurrounded by ssserpents and shrouded in evil intent. The ssstories you might have heard about The Sssnake Pit were true. When one livesss only to torment and feassst upon the innocent, you forget that the sssun shinesss. You fall ignorant to the fact that happinesss could possibly even exissst.

"For weeks, I've watched over this farm. I've ssseen how you work together, how you ressspect one another. My brother wasss right. On your cherished groundsss there isss no reassson to be treacherous. I do not except to be forgiven for all of my atrocitiesss, and I fully expect to live until my final hoursss in the prison that is the kingdom of the snakesss. I sssimply wished to sssee my brother once more and tell him... I'm sssorry..."

Sick looked down at Chake and bowed his head in respect. As he slid his way across the barn floor, Chake asked him to stop.

"Sick. Stay."

Sick looked back.

"I don't belong here, my brother."

"Everyone belongs here, Sick," CC stepped in and spoke. "On this farm, we don't care who you are or what you look like. As long as you do your part, you have a home here."

Everyone in the barn agreed.

"I mean, you might want to change your name, but yeah, we're all family here," CC joked.

"So, what do you say?" Chake asked his brother.

"Wait! What's he going to eat?" chimed in the high-pitched voice of a mouse named Vega.

"Actually, I've never eaten a living creature. While I've ssscared many with my impending bite, it was only used to frighten. I have a sssnakes ability to terrify, but a chickens ssstomach. I much prefer grain."

Everyone let out a sigh of relief.

"Chake, will you have me here?" Sick asked.

"Without a doubt, my brother. Welcome home!"

The two brothers embraced as the rest of the Farm Community cheered. The Farm gained a new member inside of their incredible new barn.

Weeks went by, and life on The Farm settled back down to normal. But compared to what it was like before the fire and before the investigation, a standard, typical, average, ordinary day was just perfect...

...or...

"Chicken Snake! Chupacabra Cow!" barked the dogs as they woke CC and Chake, as well as "Snick," which Sick was now known as.

"Hurry!" the begging dogs yelled through the fences.

"What's the problem?" CC asked.

"It's The Farmer! He's missing!"

CC, Chake & Snick all looked at each other. They all adjusted their ties, and CC snapped out his notebook. The next investigation has begun!

ACKNOWLEDGMENTS

So much has changed since this book was written. Brandon Jr. has grown up and is heading out on his own path. Brandon Sr. is currently traveling across the nation filming television shows, etc.. Still, one thing that has not changed is how much this father loves his son. We may not see each other as much, and we may not talk as much, but I truly hope he knows that I will always be there, no matter the distance.

After years of TV shows, books, and endless adventures, this book represents the last project we've done together, and it means more than this writer can put into words.

Thanks to my daughter Charlotte and grandson Chance for coming into this realm. I cannot wait to see where it all goes from here. The next book needs to be one that we all write together. Love you people!

Thank you to my mom for always supporting me, no matter how insane or outlandish my endeavors may be. You are an amazing person, a success story, and my favorite person walking the planet.

Thank you to Ron for taking care of my mom all these years. She deserves a wonderful partner in life, and I'm so glad she found you.

Thank you to Logan and Leanne, Dale and Jennifer for being wonderful influences on my son. The hardest thing I've ever done is stepping back and watching him travel his own route, but I know he's in the best of places.

RIP, Marci J Cat, for 19 years, you were my longest constant. Most of this book was written with you on my lap. I know cats can't read, especially ghost cats, but thank you nonetheless.

Thank you to Gary Lee Vincent and Solon Tsangaras for being the machine behind releasing this book and other books. Not to mention our movies, music, and more. It takes a village, and I'm glad you're both my neighbors. Also, thank you to Vinnie Vineyard for bringing us all together. Here's to years of creativity and productivity.

And thank you to everyone whose eyeballs have graced the pages of this wacky, silly, ridiculous book. We had a blast writing it; my son came up with the names of different animals, and I put it all together with a story.

For all the parents out there, do this: create something with your kids, spend that time with them so you can have something to look back on and hold onto. No matter where my son and I end up, we will always have this book and the time we spent making it. There's nothing better than that!

ABOUT THE AUTHOR

Brandon. Bishop Sr. - Owner of ASY TV (asytv.com), TV Host of *Go There Eat That*, *Travel Magnetic*, *ASY TV Vanlife*, former pro wrestler, singer for One Eyed Buffalo, film director, actor, retired US Army, Radio Host of *Everything on this Small Blue Dot Podcast*, Author of *Go There Eat That: Road Stories & Recommendations*, *Billy Fred Whopper Goggles*, and *Why the 80's Were Awesome/Awful*, (2024).

www.ingramcontent.com/pod-product-compliance
Lightning Source LLC
Chambersburg PA
CBHW070942250626
47159CB00009B/3357